To Have and to Hold

Terri Mackenzie

Book Cover by Getcovers

Also by Terri Mackenzie

Finders Keepers

In Search of a Hero

To Marry the Devil

The Picture of Desire

His Ample Desire

To Have and to Hold

Contents

Prologue

April 1812

Miss Cecily Wexford's mother pinched her arm, shoving her towards the pianoforte. "Go," she hissed. "Play for them. And impress them."

Cecily stared at the man seated by the piano. His fingers danced over the keys as though he had born playing the instrument and would go to his grave with the ability intact. His hazel eyes met hers from across the room, and he gave her encouraging smile. Although some of the other ladies had whispered about him, the handsome baronet with a fortune to his name, she had never understood his appeal. For one thing, he must have around twenty years on her—and she supposed that if he had remained unmarried for that long, he had little incentive to marry now. For another, he had none of the dashing manners that a certain *other* young gentleman she knew did.

Still, in the months of her debut, he had been unfailingly kind to her, dancing with her whenever she found herself short of a partner, and always going out of his way to make conversation with her. She knew how lucky she was to have such a kind friend when navigating society sometimes seemed like balancing on a razor's edge.

"Miss Wexford," he said lightly, rising from his place at the pianoforte. "I'm delighted that you've come to join me. Please say you will elevate my performance to something that might please the masses."

She smiled shyly at him. "The masses, I think, have been well pleased."

"Then they are sure to be transported when you sing."

"You cannot know that."

"On the contrary," he said, gesturing her into the seat and handing her a sheaf of music. "I had the pleasure of hearing you at Lady Wimbledon's soiree. A rarer voice I've not heard."

"Now I *know* you're just trying to make me feel better." She lowered herself into the seat and examined the music. Her face still felt a little flushed. Coming to the capitol from their home in the country had proven a shock; now, she was expected to not only entertain her family, an ancient squire who drooled as he slept, and the local vicar, but an entire room of the *ton*. All of whom watched her with somewhat bored interest.

"Is it working?" He smiled down at her as he turned the page to a Scottish air. *Robin Adair*, one of her favourites.

"I—yes." She rubbed her arm absently from where her mother had pinched her. Tomorrow, she knew, she would have a bruise, but at least her gloves would cover the mark. "But only because I know you'll sing with me."

"As you wish."

"Would you like to select a duet?"

"Not at all. This will suit you nicely, and I'm certain I can rustle up a harmony from somewhere."

Just like him, she had heard him sing before. He had a rich tenor that made something stir in her chest, similar to when she had attended the theatre and heard Angelica Catalani sing.

Her music master had once told her that music was the food of the soul, and she wondered if Sir Percy's soul felt as hungry as hers always did when she attempted to play. As though she could not push hard enough to capture the transient beauty of the music—it was too fleeting, however desperately she attempted to commit it to the world. Once the last note faded, it had gone forever. The thought made her ache in a strange way, and she rested her fingers on the keys, taking a breath.

Then she began to play.

Since attending the capitol, the hunger in her soul had turned to something else—a desire not just for beauty but for love. Specifically, love from the man whose dark eyes watched her so hungrily from his position in the corner. No lady could meet William Devereaux and emerge unscathed. Her heart, certainly, had been affected by his languid compliments, the burn of something unholy in his eyes when he looked at her, and the possessive way he had taken her hand for their dances together. Surely he would offer for her soon, and her life with him would be complete.

Beside her, Sir Percy began to sing, and Cecily's preoccupation with William briefly turned course. How odd that a man otherwise so old and staid could have such a beautiful voice. It blended with hers, rising and falling, soaring effortlessly as he wove intricate harmonies around her melody. Apparently he had meant it when he'd said that he could rustle up a harmony.

The corner of his mouth quirked as he glanced down at her, and for a moment, she forgot that he was so much older than her, practically her father, and that she had plans to marry William. For a moment, the world held nothing but the two of them and this song bridging the distance between, shimmering in the air like thread.

The song ended, the music stopped, and just as it always did, it faded into nothing, taking the sense of belonging that came with it. Cecily rose, curtsied to Sir Percy, and thanked him for elevating her performance. Then she retreated from the pianoforte in search of William.

For the longest time, Cecily could not find William, and it was only as she lingered by the half-open door leading into the gardens that she finally spied him, illuminated by the lights from the house.

"You were magnificent," he said, coming forward and taking her hand at once. "Come, take a turn with me. I find the cool air is most refreshing after the stuffiness of the house."

She laughed uncertainly. "The house isn't stuffy."

"Well then, perhaps it's that I would rather be alone with you, petal. Somewhere your mother's eyes are not always on us."

How delightful. This might finally be the moment she received her first kiss, and perhaps even a marriage proposal with it. No wonder he wanted no prying eyes on her—and especially not those of her mother. Cecily knew how little her mother encouraged romantic thoughts in . . . well, anyone.

"Just for a little while," she said, mindful of her reputation.

"Of course." He took her hand, leading her deeper into the shadows of the garden. The space was not large, surrounded by a large hedge, but nevertheless, he found a walkway with a small stone bench that could not be seen from the house.

"Now I have you all to myself," he said with some satisfaction. "Come here, petal."

She lost no time in obeying, staring up into his face. He was so very handsome, and he had flirted with her for so many months. Surely, he would declare himself.

"Do you love me?" he asked.

She hesitated. The truthful answer was *no*, or at least not yet. But she thought she certainly *could*, and she most definitely wanted to, so she nodded. "I—I think so."

"You think so? Evidently I have not been charming you enough." He lifted one of her curls from her neck, toying with it absently, and she flushed. "I have a great many plans for you, petal. But I suspect you will need to love me first. Would a kiss tip the balance in my favour, do you think?" He tilted her chin up to his, and his eyes appeared to crackle with that same fire she had seen in them before. Not warmth, the way she had seen in Sir Percy's eyes, but something entirely more scorching. Liable to burn her.

"Will you apply to my mother after?" she asked breathlessly.

He barked a laugh. "Your mother? My flower, *your* permission is all I need, I think."

This was most definitely not how she had imagined his declaration going, but he bent and kissed her, and all thoughts of propriety went out of her head. His mouth was warm and demanding, almost frightening in its roughness as he gripped her wrist a little too tightly. Right where her mother had pinched her. She opened her eyes to protest, but he broke away and shook his head.

"Say nothing, else someone will discover us together."

That *would* be bad, she supposed, but if they were going to marry anyway, she didn't think it mattered quite as much as he was making out. Either way, his arms tightened around her enough that she struggled to breathe, and as he forcibly kissed her again, she could hardly have made a noise if she had wanted to. Not that she did. He dominated every sense, forcing her into submission, and she yielded.

So this is what kissing is like.

Once she had a little more practice, she suspected she would know better what to do, and although she did enjoy this—quite a lot, actually, her body buzzing under his—she suspected she would enjoy it more once she knew what to do with her hands. Where did one put one's hands during a first kiss? He held her jaw and her wrist, and after some internal debate, she rested her hands lightly on his lapels.

That had evidently been the right thing to do, because he made a noise of approval. “You will look so pretty bare before me,” he said, and she wanted to argue that in all the ways that mattered, she *had* bared herself before him. But before she could say anything further, his body ripped from hers. She cried out, this time in shock rather than pleasure, as a shadow took William’s lapels, the same she had been holding, and his fist encountered William’s handsome, perfect face.

Chapter One

June 1816

Lady Cecily Somerville stared at Sir Percy Somerville from the other side of the darkened opera house. A tenor began to sing, but although Cecily usually delighted in the opera, in music of all kinds, she found herself unable to concentrate on anything except the sight of her husband.

Her husband, specifically, with another woman.

Cecily knew of Caroline Spenser the way all ladies know of a notorious mistress of the *ton*—reluctantly, and with a good deal of misgiving. And she, like all ladies of the *ton*, felt a sudden burst of protective spirit towards her husband.

No, protective wasn't quite the right word. Wrathful, more like. Both that Caroline Spenser made advances towards her husband, and that he seemed more than amenable to these advances.

It was not that Cecily wanted Sir Percy for herself. She had never wanted him to marry her—and when he had, he had stolen her away from the only man she might ever have loved—but she certainly did not want to watch him fawn over *another* lady. He always told her that he had eyes only for her. And she had believed him, because he could have had anybody, and he had chosen her, even after discovering her in another man's embrace.

Now this. Her. *Caroline.* A voluptuous beauty with whom Cecily, all sharp angles, could never compare.

Percy bent over Caroline's hand with his signature grace, the strands of silver in his hair glinting in the candlelight, and laughed a little. Cecily ground her teeth. Even she had to admit that he looked uncommonly good that night. More so than usual, which could no doubt be attributed to the lady by his side. Who also, though Cecily didn't want to admit it, was in good looks. Percy was not the first man to be ensnared with her; he would not be the last.

And Cecily was forced to watch the humiliation unfurl for herself.

She turned to the young gentleman by her side with a wide smile. After Percy had irritated her once again, she had persuaded Lord Featherstone to issue her an invitation to the opera. But, apparently, that was where his devotion ended. At the steel in her expression, the poor boy looked almost terrified, as though her tongue were sharp enough to cut them both.

No matter. Whether or not the thought petrified him, she would find a way of flirting. Then, if Percy ever glanced over at her—which, to her precise knowledge, he had not yet done—then he would see her engrossed in her much younger companion.

"I love the opera. Don't you?" She tossed her head, knowing her ringlets bobbed, knowing they glowed in the light. Candlelight was where she excelled; it gave her pale skin the semblance of colour, glossed over her freckles, and brought out a burnished light to her hair. In daylight, she appeared like any other small, pale, freckled young lady attempting to match up to the beauty standards of the *ton.*

In candlelight, she *gleamed.*

"I—" he began.

"It's so romantic. And the singing is always divine."

He barely glanced at the stage. "I suppose so. I prefer seeing what everyone else is doing."

"What else could anyone be doing?" Her laugh grated on her own ears. Heavens, she wanted nothing more than to go home to bed. The only reason she had put in an appearance here had been because Percy had smothered her in unwanted attention when she'd been trying to go elsewhere, implying that she needed his escort. As though any lady wanted a husband pestering her at all hours of the day.

Thus, she had punished him.

But instead of showing some chagrin, he'd taken the opportunity to showcase his mistress to the world.

"Would you not rather pay what's inside your box more attention than what's out there?" she asked finally, desperate for Lord Featherstone to look at her. "I would have thought that might prove more interesting."

He sent her a quick, scared glance. "My mother is here somewhere."

"Oh to be a boy tied to his mother's apron strings," she muttered, quietly enough that he didn't hear her over the crescendoing screech of the violins. Her head throbbed, and her temper threatened to soar out of control.

Biting back her frustration, she continued to flirt outrageously until the intermission, during which time she spoke to a variety of acquaintances, and pretended she didn't notice their pitying looks.

Of course, it was not so very unusual for a gentleman to have a lover—or for him to flaunt her to the world. But Percy had been so very constant, had given every impression of a devoted husband—to the extent that it had been stifling. So to see him here meant people would draw their own conclusions. No doubt that Cecily's first blush of youth had faded, her beauty diminishing after four years of marriage, and he had lost interest. Bored, he'd turned his gaze elsewhere.

Perhaps the assumption was *right.* After all, he looked cosy enough with Caroline, and he hadn't spared a single glance for Cecily. Perhaps he had tired of her. *Good riddance.* But he should not have behaved so publicly. People would talk—were already talking, whispering behind their fans and painted smiles.

Poor Lady Somerville.

They always do turn, in the end, even the good ones.

I'd thought he adored the girl. Pity!

She hated every one of their poisoned words. But instead of going home, as she wanted, she returned to Lord Featherstone's box, even though they both knew he would rather she didn't. And there, for the first time, she saw the empty box opposite where Percy and Caroline had sat. They had gone. No doubt they were having a delightful tryst together somewhere.

Delightful, strictly, for them. Cecily did not feel delightful at all.

In fact, she felt positively murderous.

Ignoring the pounding in her head and the sickening twist in her stomach, she turned her attention to the stage and allowed Lord Featherstone to lapse into silence beside her. And although she knew there were whispers aimed at her from all directions, she smiled and put on the best performance of her life to persuade them that she cared about nothing and no one but her own transient, fleeting pleasures.

Sir Percy Somerville strolled along the quiet, empty road towards his home on Harley Street, his cane in one hand and an armful of regret in the other. The night was still, mist gathering by the lamps in soft tendrils, and damp gathered on his fine woollen coat. Really, he ought to have called for his carriage. The walk had been to clear his head, but he wasn't drunk, just a fool.

And, if he was honest, he was dreading the confrontation that would arise when he finally arrived home. He estimated the opera would be reaching its zenith; soon after, she would be following him, in the carriage. Then he would have all the leisure in the world in which to regret his decisions. There were plenty. In no particular order he had: pretending to the world and his wife that he had a mistress; attending the opera with said mistress—a notorious lady he had no feelings for; marrying his wife.

Perhaps there was an order.

Perhaps his marriage was at the top of the list.

Of course, that operated under the assumption that she would return home that night at all. He kept no tabs on her, mostly because he knew how much of her freedom he'd taken away—or at least, had appeared to—when he'd arranged for their marriage. And that meant that he truly did not know how many lovers she had, if she had any at all. Her disinclination to lie with him could be attributed to dislike of him rather than inexperience or chastity.

Impossible to know. Impossible to tell.

Utterly impossible to ignore or forget.

His house came into view. With a sigh, half wishing he was drunk, he ascended the steps and rapped on the door with the head of his cane. His valet hurried to open it, and not for the first time, Percy wondered what the poor man must think.

"Would you like to retire for the night, sir?" he asked as Percy entered and relinquished his cane.

Why not? If he and Cecily were going to argue, perhaps it was less dignified to do so in a dressing gown, but he couldn't bring himself to care. At least he would be comfortable.

"Very well," he said. "I'm anticipating Lady Somerville will be home shortly."

"Yes, sir."

Percy made his way to the dressing room he shared with Cecily—although *shared* was an optimistic term for a couple who shared very little in their lives, and certainly not their bed—and undressed, wrapping a robe around his shoulders as he sat by the fire. He picked up a book to pass the time, turning the pages idly.

Less than an hour later, Cecily flounced in, her curls dishevelled but her dress perfectly in place. He skimmed over her appearance, noting all the ways in which he considered it unlikely that she had been even remotely ravished.

His heart, foolish thing that it was, leapt.

At the sight of him sitting there waiting for her, she halted partway into the room. Her mouth fell open, and her chest rose and fell with several unsteady breaths.

"Percy," she said, and appeared to gather herself. She cocked a brow. "Home already? I hadn't expected that of you."

"Evidently not."

"I assumed you would be spending the night elsewhere."

He folded the book carefully, careful to preserve the pages without a crease. Originally, he had intended to allow this deception to continue, but now he knew he could not. Both for his sake and hers; he was not built for lying.

"Caroline is not my mistress," he said, enunciating the words so there could be no confusion. "We are friends."

"And you expect me to believe that? You left together."

That had been because Caroline had wanted to conduct an assignation of her own, and he could not bear the idea of sitting alone in his box, watching his wife flirt with another.

"We went our separate ways." He gestured at himself. "As you can see."

"All I see is a husband who humiliated me tonight." She tossed her head. "I have a headache and I have no wish to continue this conversation. Goodbye, Percy." She turned on her heel and stalked towards her bedchamber.

"Busy, were you?" The words broke free before he intended them to.

Her back stiffened, and she turned with menacing grace. She had always been beautiful, with her auburn curls and flashing peridot eyes, but she could also be terrifying. "Well," she said with cold intent. "Perhaps I was. Does that offend your sensibilities?"

"As a matter of fact, it does."

"Why? Are you allowed to stray while I remain at home, warming the marital bed?" Her mouth thinned, and he thought of how much he wanted to kiss it. The likelihood of her allowing him to was low indeed.

"As I said, Caroline and I are merely friends."

Her eyes glittered. "Is that so? I have yet to see mere friends as close as the two of you appeared tonight."

Well, that had been the purpose of the display: to incite jealousy.

Success had never tasted so bitter.

"It seems you know a lot about the subject," he said, pushing himself out of his chair. "Tell me more about your companion. Lord Featherstone, was it? The boy's barely out of Oxford."

"I prefer associating with *contemporaries*." She layered the word with such meaning that he practically flinched. Yes, he knew he'd taken a risk in marrying a spirited lady so much his junior, and she never let him forget it.

"Are you fond of him?" he asked.

"Does it matter to you? Are you *fond* of Caroline Spenser?"

"As a friend, yes."

"Oh, certainly. One of the *ton's* most notorious mistresses, a close friend. How likely. Do you think me a fool?"

When he'd dreamt up his ridiculous plan, he'd had vague intentions of using her anger to bring them closer together. Somehow, he had envisioned that it would inspire intimacy. Now, with his wife fiercely beautiful, and unmistakeably furious, he didn't know what he had been thinking. Desperation had made him delusional.

"I think," he said, giving way to honesty, "you are selfish."

"Excuse me?"

"And, my darling, a trifle hypocritical. Either you were entertaining your escort intending to make him your lover—in which case, you can hardly object to me doing the same—or you meant nothing by it, in which case, why not think me capable of the same?"

Her eyes darkened and her nostrils flared, and he wished he did not think her quite so frighteningly lovely when she was on the verge of losing her temper entirely.

"You *humiliated* me," she repeated. "Where everyone might see. Does my reputation mean nothing to you?"

"And what of mine? Does it not suffer too?"

"You are *impossible.*" Jaw set, she flounced from the room. And he, a glutton for punishment, followed. "People saw you with her, and they *pitied* me. What do you suppose they thought? That you and Caroline were merely friends?" Her hands shook as she attempted to unfasten her earrings. "You *left* with her."

"I came straight home. Here, let me." He caught her wrist, setting it aside as he applied himself to the task of removing her earrings, which had become caught in her curls.

"It doesn't *matter*. Don't you understand? People will have seen the empty box, and I think we both know what conclusions they came to."

"Does their opinion matter more than yours and mine?" He turned her by her slim shoulders so he might remove the other earring. Two rubies, glistening in his palms like drops of blood. He closed his fingers around them. "Be honest with me, Cecily."

She stiffened even before she turned to face him. "Honesty is rarely redeemed in this marriage."

"Is it not?" Gently, with the fingers of one hand, he tilted her face to his. "Then let me be honest first. I wasn't sure you would even notice I was with Caroline tonight."

Her pupils swelled, eating into the vibrant colour of her iris, even as she reared back, wrenching her chin from his hand. "Why? Because I have so little pride?"

Because she had never wanted him as a husband.

"Because I didn't think you cared," he said. "Now tell me something—is this to be the state of affairs for the rest of our lives? Are you going to deny me the companionship of others while denying me the same at home? Am I to return to an empty house every night because my wife has found more entertainment elsewhere, and wishes me to have no part in it?"

Her steps faltered as she crossed to her dressing table. "No husband acts as a constant escort to his wife. It's unbecoming."

"Few wives are so independent."

"Untrue! Why, I know several ladies who—" With visible difficulty, she bit off the words. "Well, it hardly matters. What would you have change, Percy?"

It had been such a long time since she had last used his name that he could almost taste its sweetness in the air.

"Everything," he said. He suddenly felt tired, the difference in age between them weighing him down. For the sake of his wellbeing, he could not continue to give her every part of himself and receive nothing in return.

"Everything?"

"We both know this isn't working."

"Oh, so now you agree that our marriage is a poor one?" She placed her hands on her hips, almost incandescent in her fury. Once, perhaps, she could have been a warrior queen. "I wish you'd made that decision before deciding behind my back that I would be better matched with you than anyone else."

He knew what she meant; better than with William Devereaux. For years, she'd persisted in the delusion that his flirtation with her had been headed towards marriage, not something entirely more ruinous. And for years, Percy had attempted to preserve her feelings, knowing that if he spoke out against the gentleman she had settled her heart on, she would not take it well.

He dropped her earrings on the dressing table. "Then we both agree things cannot continue as they are. You barely tolerate my presence, and I'm exhausted of always being the one trying to make it right. Yes, I accepted your parents' proposal when they offered it. I thought I could bring you to love me with time and patience. Now, I see I was mistaken." He met her gaze. "*Am* I mistaken, Cecily?"

She swallowed, but she gave no answer. That was answer enough.

"I see." With some difficulty, he kept the hurt from his voice. "So, then, let us change our arrangement."

"How?"

"You do not want a husband; by law, I cannot change that, but in actions I will. If my presence offends you, then I will lodge elsewhere. And when you retire to the country at the end of the Season, I will not join you."

She was utterly motionless. Shadows crept over her, casting her into darkness. If he could turn back time, he would free her from this abominable thing they called a life together. As he could not, he would do the next best thing.

"Where will you live?" she asked.

"I will arrange for my things to be packed up and redirected to my lodgings in Town."

"That—" She drew in a breath, the column of her neck tensing with the movement. "That won't be necessary. People will talk."

"Let them."

"No." Instinctively, she reached out to lay a hand on his arm. When he glanced down, she snatched her hand away. "That is, I would rather they didn't. After the incident tonight . . . If my mother hears about the situation, she will . . ."

Percy knew exactly what she would do.

Her mother was a widowed viscountess, and she delighted—with, what he felt, could only be sadistic pleasure—in making the people around her as miserable as possible. If she knew there were issues in their marriage—one which she had arranged with such eagerness, securing for herself a fat settlement in the process, then she would be sure to descend. And yes, he could refuse her entry into his house, but she outranked him, and she could cause all sorts of unpleasantness he would rather avoid.

Even so, he disliked this halfway house. It would be difficult to avoid her in the same house—but what better way to protect his maimed heart than to steer clear from the thing that continued to break it? He could not continue to withstand the pain of her rejection; it was beyond endurance. If there had been any other way forward that he could see . . . But he could not. Short of forcing her, which he would and could not do, little else remained to be done.

"Very well," he said. "I will continue to live here. But our lives are to be separate. Do you understand?"

Her nostrils flared, and he thought she would argue. A not insignificant part of him *wished* she would argue, fighting for the marriage she had never asked for. Instead, she merely said, "Do you have anything else to say to me, or may I retire to bed now?"

He didn't know why he'd bothered to hope.

"Goodnight, Cecily." He bowed, as though she were a stranger he was meeting for the first time, and retired from her bedchamber into his own. There, he did his best to feel as though the night had been a victory.

Chapter Two

Cecily slipped her arm through that of her best friend, Mrs Arabella Sandhurst. They'd met during Cecily's first season, and had both married at similar times. Arabella to the penniless second son of an earl, whom she loved, and Cecily to her baronet, whom she didn't.

They didn't always promenade in Hyde Park, but Arabella had insisted, dragging Cecily out in her best walking dress. And instead of the grey pelisse Cecily had reached for, Arabella had insisted on a deep emerald one, delicately laced.

"It brings out your eyes," she'd said.

Cecily, all too happy to look her best, had tied the buttons with a smile. Now Percy had effectively relinquished his claim on her, she had a sense of freedom. Now, more than ever, she could do as she wished. More than that—he *wanted* her to.

He had asked to be separate. Finally, after four years of wishing, he had given in. And so Cecily had chosen her most fetching bonnet. Perhaps she would find a new beau to flirt with.

Arabella certainly seemed to think she would.

"What is this surprise you have for me?" she asked now, tilting her head so her bonnet shielded her face from the sun. The very last thing she needed was to encourage *more* freckles across her nose.

Arabella laughed, her plump face glowing. "That defeats the object of the surprise."

"Whom are we to meet? I presume that's why you brought me here."

"You should not be so observant."

Seizing her opening, Cecily mentioned how observant she had been at the opera—what she had seen, and what the outcome of that had been.

"How cruel he was to humiliate you!" Arabella said, indignant in a way that spoke of her own love for her husband, who would never have stooped to such tricks. Then again, *she* would never have flirted with Lord Featherstone as a form of revenge.

After consideration, perhaps she and Percy were both as bad as one another.

Regardless, it was better they no longer lived as husband and wife.

"It's not so bad," Cecily said, patting Arabella's hand. "Of course, he should not have done it so publicly, but I don't think he will do so again, and it's hardly as though I sought his affection. Why should I care if he bestows it on another?"

"Odd that I never heard of Caroline Spenser's name being linked to his. I'd have thought, if they were openly seeing one another, I would have heard something."

"You do not have *all* the gossip."

"I assure you, if I don't know it, it is not worth knowing. I have the ear of the Dowager Duchess of Norfolk, and she is a formidable creature. She confides in me. The rest, my husband gleans from his fellow officers. So, you see, I know everything. I could tell you all the names of Caroline Spenser's former lovers."

Cecily waved a hand; she had no desire to know anything further about Caroline Spenser. "My point is, he will no longer be attempting to win me over, and I have the freedom to live my life as I wish without having to endure his attentions."

"Do you intend to find a lover?" Arabella asked curiously.

"No! At least, I don't know. I don't think so." She touched the ring on her finger, concealed by her glove. When Percy made his announcement, she'd considered taking it off. Not all ladies wore rings—and most gentlemen did not. More bound them together than a sliver of gold. Still, she kept it on, and she rubbed it as she spoke. "I'm not interested in finding anyone else."

Arabella twinkled at her. "*No* one else? I can think of at least one gentleman who caught your eye."

"When we were children," Cecily said with as much dignity as she could muster, although four years ago felt like both a blink of an eye and a lifetime when it came to a broken heart. Well, perhaps not a broken heart. She had not precisely *loved* him, but she'd thought she might. And whenever she thought of Percy's shortcomings, she found that the largest one she could think of pertained to the fact he was not William Devereaux.

"What if," Arabella said with false solemnity, "I told you that you have another chance at charming the infamous Mr Devereaux?"

Cecily turned, thoughts of Percy forgotten. William had left England for the continent shortly after Percy had found them together, and she hadn't seen him since. Not when her mother had announced she had arranged a marriage with Sir Percy, and certainly not when the same man—after stealing her every chance of happiness—had the gall to expect her to fall in love with him. As though her heart were a berry ripe for the plucking by any gentleman who might come along, rather than a sacred thing saved for the man she thought the best of.

All this time, she had not seen the one man she'd always supposed she would give her heart to.

"He's returned?" she asked.

"While you were witnessing your husband's betrayal, I was receiving the latest updates from my friend Miss Patricia Helmsworth, and—"

"Don't tease me! What did you discover?"

"Why, that your dear William had returned from Italy and has been in London these two weeks since. I came this morning with the intention of seeing if we could find him. I've heard that he sometimes rides out in the morning. Or perhaps he will walk. Either way, if he's here, then we will find him. *And* if you mean what you say about your situation with Sir Percy . . ." Arabella sucked on her lip. "Far be it from me to encourage any unwifely behaviour, but perhaps you could put this newfound freedom of yours to good use when you see him. Not, I suspect, that your husband could have stopped you if you had chosen to do so before."

No, Percy certainly could not have stopped her. But although she'd had plenty of flirts, and more than one gentleman had presumed that because she was easy with her smiles she would be easy with her other favours, they had all discovered she was not.

This, however, was entirely different. A matter of the heart, not of the body.

William Devereaux, finally back from his self-imposed exile.

"Weeks?" she said. "He has been here for weeks and hasn't come to call on me?"

"Why should he, dearest? You're a married lady now."

The ring on her finger burned.

William had returned.

"Come on," she said, hurrying forwards and dragging Arabella behind her. "Let's see if we can find him."

They had walked the full stretch of Hyde Park and were on the verge of giving up and returning home when Arabella stood on her tiptoes. "I think I see him!"

Cecily felt as though something had launched itself at her stomach. A brick, perhaps, or a particularly heavy flowerpot.

The wind blew again, tossing her hair into her eyes, and she reached a hand up to clear her vision. By the time she had, she was face to face with a tall, handsome man. One she remembered from her dreams.

He looked as dashing as he'd been the day they had met, a little over four years ago, when she'd come to London dreaming of a great love. Dark eyes, raven hair loosely brushed back from his forehead, and a smile that curved so wickedly, she felt her heartbeat increase.

Yet there were differences, too. Creases around his mouth that didn't speak of smiles so much as dissipation, and premature lines across his forehead. He wasn't so very much older than her, perhaps twenty-five or twenty-six, but it was as though she could map the time they'd been apart across his features.

His gaze passed across her face, and Cecily swallowed, her throat suddenly dry. She'd imagined this day so many times—imagined Percy having perished of an unmentioned ailment so that when they met again, she was a merry widow. Reality, however, rendered her girlish fantasies somewhat sour.

She was not a merry widow, and nor did she want to be. Percy may not be the husband of her dreams, and she certainly did not like him much, but she'd never wish death on him.

William, too . . . Well, in her fantasies, he had stayed the same as he always had been, but now he stood before her, she saw how ridiculous that assumption had been.

"Well I'll be," he said, taking her hand and bending over it with a graceful flourish. "Can it be Cecily Wexford?"

"Cecily Somerville now," she said, taking her hand back. Her heart felt as though it was pummelling her ribcage. The sight of him, all the feelings she'd once had, come to attack her once more.

"Ah yes, of course. You married the baronet. My felicitations."

"Thank you." She looked into his face, and it felt as though he, too, were assessing her. Arabella joined William's companion, and they all fell in together, walking along the promenade as they had once done over four years ago. "What has brought you back to London?" she asked.

"Merely that I felt I had been away from it too long. And, of course, away from certain ladies." He inclined his head in her direction, and familiar warmth spilled over her. This was how it had been when they were together—he had always contrived to make her feel so special. A heady, almost desperate rush, sweeping her along in its tide. "Tell me, how are you?"

What a complex question. "Well."

"Is that so? And what of your husband—does he treat you 'well'?"

Aside from the opera, where she could concede she had behaved just as poorly, the answer could hardly be a negative. Of course, she hadn't cared for his good treatment, and if she could have chosen, she might almost have wished he'd treat her badly, so she had more reason to hate him. As it was, all she could find to say was, "Yes, of course."

"Hardly a surprise. I saw first-hand how very ardent he was."

Cecily glanced around them, wishing she could loosen her dress to breathe more easily, though her stays were not tight. "We do not have to talk about him."

"Indeed not. Now we have the pleasantries out of the way, shall we talk about you? You are looking ravishingly lovely today."

"You seem to have come back a greater flatterer, sir," she said, hiding a smile.

He doffed his hat at a passing young lady. "Do you think? Well, I'm glad. It's my greatest pleasure to flatter young ladies—particularly when everything I say is God's honest truth. You are one of the most beautiful ladies I've ever had the pleasure of conversing with."

"Now I *know* you're lying."

"No, how could you say such a thing? You have always had such power over me. You could strike me down with a single look."

She laughed. "I very much doubt that. So much time has passed."

"Has it? It feels like a day, an hour. Barely a minute has passed since I was last in your company." He gave her another wickedly slow smile. "No, but I must be honest with you. I am more than a little grateful we met in this way. I'd hoped to encounter you again upon returning to London, and finding you in such rare beauty is an additional blessing."

"Had you anticipated seeing me ugly?"

"I'd convinced myself nothing could compare to the image of you I have in my mind. Utterly divine. Spectacularly lovely. And yet it transpires my imagination could not do you justice."

She tilted her head, even as her heart gave another flip. Not the same flutter as it might have done four years ago, but a taste of former joy. She'd once lived for compliments like these, far more outrageous than the ones Percy had ever given her. No, he had always spoken about her as though her feet rested firmly on the ground. William spoke about her as though she were an angel.

"You are a shocking flirt," she said, attempting severity.

"Why, am I? Surely it's only because the temptation is so great. I defy any gentleman to spend time with you and *not* do so."

"You've only just seen me again after four years apart."

"Four painful years, I assure you. If you think I have forgotten, let me assure you I have not. I think about you every night." This time, the smile he offered her appeared distinctly lascivious. "I think about all that might have happened if we were not discovered."

"Yes," she said, and sighed. That kiss *had* been lovely. "To think, if we had not been discovered and if Percy had not led you away, you might have had a chance to propose."

A hesitation, more like a heartbeat, passed between the end of her words and the beginning of his next. "Never mind what might have been—we can still consider what can still be. I have a proposition for you, petal. There's a masquerade at the Pantheon next week. Let me escort you."

A brief surge of the reckless, heady feeling she'd once experienced with him suffused her, and she smiled, curling the hand with her ring into a fist. "Very well," she said. "I look forward to it."

Chapter Three

Cecily returned home with her nerves fluttering. After meeting William, she had gone shopping with Arabella, who wanted desperately to know what Cecily intended to do about her old beau, but Cecily hadn't been able to answer her.

The problem was, she hardly knew herself. Yes, he was terribly, dashingly handsome, just the same as always. And she had always assumed that he would be the only man she ever loved. Seeing him again had been like a fresh of fresh air. The situation with Percy being as it was, she might be well be able to have a lover, if she wanted him—and if he would consent to being hers.

The thought almost disturbed her. Certainly, she had flirted often, and with great enjoyment, but she had never considered breaking her marriage vows in that direction.

Then again, she had never been adequately persuaded. And William, she fancied, could be extremely persuasive if he put his mind to it. Just thinking about the way he had treated her upon seeing her again proved that; he was just as much of a flirt as ever, and evidently hoped that he might find himself in favour with her once more. Perhaps he had never fallen out of love with her, and he hoped for . . .

What, was the question. There was no chance of him marrying her now. Would he be satisfied with being her lover?

Would she?

The sight of Percy in the hallway jolted her from her thoughts, and she started. At the sight of her, and her surprise, his lips thinned. "Cecily," he said, his tone reserved. "Fear not—I was on my way out."

"Where?"

He raised both brows. "Is it of your concern?"

"No," she said immediately. Perhaps this was a good thing. Now she would have time to think, and come to a conclusion about what she would do about William. Still, she knew she looked unwell, flushed and bright-eyed and out of breath, though she had done nothing particularly strenuous. She waited for Percy to ask about her wellbeing, to pry until he had the answers from her, ripped from her tongue, no matter how unwilling she was to let him in.

Instead, he merely looked at her face, frowned, then picked up his cane and turned to the door. She froze, her expectancy dissolving into . . . surprise.

Yes, that was it. Surprise. Certainly not disappointment, given that she had no intention of telling Percy about William.

"Will you be out for dinner?" she blurted, and he turned from the doorway.

"I imagine so. I'd say not to wait up, but I know you won't." With a nod that felt better suited to a casual acquaintance than to a wife, he left the house.

"Shall I take these packages upstairs, my lady?" her footman asked, nodding to the boxes still in his arms.

Absently, she nodded and followed him up. Once in her dressing room, she sank onto the sofa as the servants put away her new purchases. All around her, the sound of the empty house felt as though it settled into her bones. She thought about Arabella, no doubt home with her handsome captain husband, sharing what Cecily knew to be a very happy life together.

She thought about William, who had seemed so pleased to see her, so ready to enter into a flirtation, and who could never truly be hers.

Then she thought about her husband. The life she'd forged for herself, better or worse.

The ring on her finger almost seemed to mock her. All the times she had wished a different man had put it there, and now he had finally arrived—too late.

Would that he had asked her to marry him instead of kissing her. He should have gone straight to her mother to ask for permission to court her. In fact, it was odd he had not. She frowned, thinking it through. For years, she had placed him on a pedestal, thinking that he was everything Percy had never been to her, but now she considered her memory of him against the man she had met that day.

Every instinct screamed at her to enter into a flirtation with him and succumb to all the feelings that had swept her away when she'd been younger. But a certain level of womanly wisdom bade her wait. He did not seem like a man who had wasted away over heartbreak, and he certainly did not appear as though he valued her above all others.

After all, he had not sought her out when he'd returned to London. That point still stung. The only reason they had met at all was by chance and Arabella's machinations. And yes, he had appeared delighted to see her, but she could not deceive herself that there was anything of the lover about him. The flirt, perhaps. But if he had ever loved her, he did no longer.

The question was whether he could love her again. And if she wanted him to.

The week passed indeterminably slowly, made worse by the fact that Percy did not join her for dinner for three nights in a row. Previously, whenever he'd been home, he had sat with her and they had made stilted small talk, but now he made no appearance.

It was not strictly unusual for them to eat separately. Often, she was the one to have left in search of more entertaining options while Percy remained at home. With the situation this way around, she found it . . . unpleasant.

Until now, she had never considered what it must have been like for him. Had he eaten here with a newspaper or one of his steward's reports? She knew he frequently made investments, though she was unsure precisely about what. It had never occurred to her to ask. Did he eat at his desk while working? Or did he lean back in his chair with a glass of port and lead everyone around him to believe he was indifferent to his situation?

After all, he had been a bachelor, living in this same house, before he had married. What difference did a marriage make when they were never with one another?

She pressed her lips together. Coming from a large and busy household, where dinner was sacred and they were all expected to eat together, she found this silence unpalatable.

Then there were the servants to consider. She wanted no one to know of this new arrangement, and she felt their eyes on her, imagined the weight of their judgement that her husband disliked her company so much that he had rather take his dinner elsewhere in the house.

Before she reached the final course, she pushed back her plate. "My compliments to the cook," she said, mechanically, as she rose and moved to the door. A footman opened it for her, and she took stock of the empty house.

She had no plans for the evening. That was the problem. If she had just found something else to distract herself with, she would never have noticed how many empty rooms Somerville House boasted. A drawing room, a music room, three small parlours, a library, a billiards room, a dining room, a morning room. All downstairs. Percy's study.

More to the point, Percy's *presence* was what irritated her the most. If he'd gone out, she could have excused his absence, but she knew he had not left, which meant he had rather eaten separately than joining her for dinner.

Unacceptable.

The restlessness bubbled over, and she made her way to his study—that indomitably male space she had never thought to breach.

Until now, that was.

If he intended to embarrass her before the servants, he would find she did not take it lightly. Dining together was not asking too much of him, and after all, when she was home, she dined with him. It was only fair he did the same for her.

Just as she suspected, when she opened his study door, he was indeed there, a candle lit before him and a half-eaten tray of food to one side. At her entrance, he glanced up, and his brows rose.

"You weren't at dinner," she said by way of greeting.

"Good evening," he said, laying down the paper he was reading. "To what can I attribute this honour?"

"Where were you?"

"I rather suspect the answer is obvious."

"You never ordinarily eat in here."

"I thought we had agreed that things were not to progress along ordinary lines." His voice was mild, but she heard the dismissal in it, and it infuriated her.

"So you let me sit and eat alone, all the servants knowing you would prefer to be separate from me?"

"I think you'll find that is hardly unusual."

"It is unusual for *us*."

"Perhaps. But I proposed we live as though we were not husband and wife and you agreed, so what else am I to do?" He picked up his quill, the tip of it brushing his chin. "You did not want a husband. Congratulations—you do not have to have one."

"And yet I am still a wife. Mistress of this house."

"Yes. Unfortunately, I cannot change that. Would you rather live elsewhere?"

At the thought of her mother descending on her, she shuddered. "I would rather we kept up appearances."

"Even inside the house?" The look he gave her now was so gently chiding, it made shame curl in the base of her stomach. "For what purpose? Your pride? My darling, you beat mine into the ground some time ago."

She knew, logically, that what he was saying made sense. She had never wanted his attention, or his tenderness. He had bestowed both on her against her will. Yet now, forced to confront the realities of that choice, she found she did not relish the idea of a life spent lonely in this house.

"You are still here," he said when he next glanced up, and there was the trace of irritation in his expression now. "What more do you have to say to me? You cannot have it both ways, Cecily. Either you welcome me as your husband, or you do not. If you do not, then why should I go out of my way to welcome you as my wife? I am not the kind of man to force you when you are unwilling, but you must allow me this freedom."

She stared at him, an unnameable emotion clawing at her throat. Anger at his dismissal, she decided. At, once again, his intention of making a decision for her.

He turned his attention back to his papers. "My mind is made up. If you would please leave me to enjoy the one room in this house which is mine, I would appreciate it."

"One room in this house? The entire property is yours."

He made a low noise in his throat—one that might have been an agreement if she didn't know him so well. Strange how even in a marriage where she had done her best to ignore him, his habits and oddities had imprinted themselves on her psyche.

Furious, both at herself and him, she whirled and slammed the door behind her. Fine—if that was how he was determined to act, then so be it. She would not stoop so low again. Forcing her to ask him to join her for dinner was the outside of enough.

Next time, she would merely not eat at home. This *was* no home for her.

She slammed every door on her way to her bedchamber, but instead of bursting into tears, which was admittedly tempting, she stormed to her vanity. What was it about Percy that brought out the very worst in her? And why, when she had never wanted his affection, never sought it, did his refusal to give any leave such a bitter taste in her mouth?

Chapter Four

It transpired that living separately from one's husband, while one's former lover made no effort to see one, proved for an unhappy existence. Cecily spent the next few days flitting from room to room, unable to find anything to entertain her for long. Percy, in their new definition of normal, now took to avoiding her at seemingly every juncture possible.

After singing at the pianoforte for a determined hour, Cecily retired to the library with a husky voice, intent on finding a book to distract her, and came up short at the sight of Percy seated before a fire that was more embers than flame.

Sunlight streamed through the half-drawn curtains, and dust motes danced in the light. Percy's head was bent, revealing the silver that streaked through his dark hair. His fingers grazed the corners of the page as he read.

For an instant, Cecily hesitated. The image before her was so decidedly domestic that she felt as though she was intruding, which was ridiculous. Yet she had never seen Percy so . . .

at peace. As though this domesticity, the quiet, was what he craved. The pads of his fingers scraped against the corner of the paper, and the sound worked something free inside her.

When they first married, she told herself she would never, under any circumstance, want him. Yet as she watched his fingers, the idleness of them, the strength in his hands even during such a mundane task, she could not help wondering what they might feel like against her skin.

A part of her hated herself for it.

A different part of herself, one dipped in desire she could not repress, burned.

It had been a very long time since he'd last visited her bed, and even then, she had made her distaste for him known, and he had left before much occurred. Until seeing him with Caroline, she had given very little thought about what that might mean for him. Whether he would find solace elsewhere, and what that form of intimacy might look like.

Now, she wondered, and she could not stop wondering.

Had he taken other women during their marriage? Did he assume she had found intimacy elsewhere also? The truth was, she had never wanted it, not with Percy or anyone else. With William, perhaps, but he had never been an option, and now the consideration made her feel uncomfortable. A coal in the base of her stomach.

Was she truly considering being unfaithful when the thought of Percy doing the same made her want to rip the curtains off the wall?

Sensing her presence, he glanced up, trapping her in his gaze, no matter how mild. Thoughts of William disintegrated, and there was a strange hollowness inside her.

Loneliness, perhaps.

She knew she should look away, but it had been such a long time since she had looked at him with the intent to *see.*

At nineteen, she had thought him old. Undesirable.

At nineteen, she supposed she had been a fool.

Something, a light, warmth perhaps, flared in Percy's eyes, but he merely said, "Did you want something? I can always leave."

"I came for a book." She advanced a little further into the room, though she made no attempt to reach for the shelves. From here, she knew, he could have heard her singing. She wondered, before she banished the thought, whether he had enjoyed it. "The light in here is pretty this time of day," she said, to distract herself.

"Oh." He looked around in apparent surprise. "Yes, it is pretty, I suppose."

"Do you often read here?"

"I did before I married," he said mildly, and returned to his book.

Irritation coursed through her, and so did her defiance—though she balked at the thought of telling him about William. "I intend to go out tomorrow evening," she announced.

He turned a page. "Is that so?"

"I went shopping especially for it."

"It certainly sounds as though you've been busy."

"Don't worry, I won't be needing an escort."

She was rewarded by the subtle tightening of his jaw. "I doubted you would." He closed the book with a snap. "Anything else?"

"I thought you might like to see my purchases. You often enjoy seeing what I spend my pin money on." She paused just long enough for him to return his gaze to her. "I bought new stockings. And garters."

His nostrils flared. "Is this designed to be punishment?"

"For what, pray?"

"I'd hoped you might inform me."

She ran her finger along the perfectly clean mantelpiece above the fire. She could hardly confess that the reason she felt so angry, so frustrated, so *alone* was in part because he left her so. "I'm bored," she said instead. "I found a new aria. I thought we might sing together. We used to, if you recall."

"I heard you practising." He looked at her steadily. "But I think I would rather read."

The blow to her chest was absurdly crushing. She hadn't practised intending to entice him to sing with her, but hearing that he had no desire to, even though it had been one of the ways he'd first courted her, sent a dizzying wave of disappointment through her.

When he'd first suggested he stop offering her his affection, she hadn't known it would mean *this.*

Percy raised his gaze to her, and she noted the green in his hazel eyes. Not dark like William's, but she found she could look into them more easily, with no danger of losing herself. "You know our arrangement, Cecily," he said gently, and rose, crossing the distance between them in two quick strides. This close, she was forced to crane her neck; the height difference was almost as vast as the difference in their ages.

"I didn't think you would refuse to talk to me at all," she said, hearing the sullenness in her voice and unable to hide it.

"I told you, my darling. You cannot have it all. I will not just take the parts of you that you choose to give." His eyes still on hers, he tucked a curl more neatly to frame her face, then dropped his hand and retreated to his seat by the fireplace. "I must return to my book. Do you need anything else?"

Her mouth was dry as she stared at him. He turned his attention to the book in his hands as though she'd never been there. Unable to articulate why the sight of that sent a pang through her, she picked up her skirts and moved towards the door. Just before he reached it, he said, the words so light they sounded like an afterthought, "You never did tell me where you were going out to."

Cecily didn't turn, though she was tempted to. Tempted to see if, when she glanced around, she would find him watching her. But that would imply that she wanted him to, and she wanted nothing less in the entire world.

Her voice was just as airy as she replied. "The Pantheon. I do love a masquerade, don't you?"

She didn't wait to hear his response.

White's was busy, and after drinking with a few of his old friends—all less invested in their wives; all happier in their marriages—Percy eventually made his way back home. Long after he was certain she was asleep, but earlier than he'd intended.

That was the problem—of many—with being in love with one's wife.

As he ascended the stairs, slowly to compensate for the spinning world, he came to their dressing room. Unlike before, the room was dark and cool, with only the faintest scent of her perfume hanging in the air.

Although he asked the servants to ensure she had already retired, some part of him was disappointed to see the lack of her. Proof that she had been; proof that she had gone.

He inhaled hungrily, and before his mind caught up with his body, he had padded to her bedchamber. The door was unlocked, and he opened it to darkness. She was asleep, buried under the covers, a shaft of moonlight piercing through the gap between curtains. He paused, aware even in his drunken state that he shouldn't be here. This was an invasion of her privacy. They might be married, but he had never forced himself on her.

But her scent was stronger here, along with all the signs of the life she led without him. Her robe tossed over the back of a chair, the book she was reading placed neatly beside her bed. Half-finished embroidery stood on a stand before the window, and sheets of paper lay on a letter-writing desk. For years, he had sought an entry into her world, and now he stood on the very brink, looking in.

Even so, the contents of her bedroom could not capture his attention for long. Not when Cecily herself lay in the bed, slumbering softly, her breathing regular. It made him ache to think how infrequently he had awoken to that sound.

This, here, was everything he had yearned for all these years. And it was just as distant as the stars.

He hadn't intended to, but he moved, striding closer, stepping around an armchair until he reached the edge of her bed. Maybe it was his presence, or maybe she heard his unsteady footsteps, because her breath halted. She stirred, raising her head. Even through the darkness, he could make out the fiery flow of her hair, loosened and softly curling around her face.

Seeing her like this was a blow to the chest. He wasn't entirely sure how he would survive it.

"Percy?" Her voice was heavy, drugged with sleep, but there was a note of alarm there, too. "Is that you?"

He should leave. Or at the very least reassure her. That was what a gentleman would do. Instead, he stayed where he was, drinking her in, wishing he had a light so he could see her all the more clearly.

"It *is* you." She made an inarticulate sound. "What are you doing there?"

Finally, he could move, but instead of leaving—as he knew he should—he approached. Closer, closer, until he could make out the darkness of her eyes, set in a pale face. By day, they were gems, but by night they were nothing but shadow. Drink made him fanciful, and he thought she resembled a faery, something otherworldly, exquisite in her beauty.

"Percy." She sounded more awake now, sitting up fully. The covers fell from her, and he could make out the swell of her breasts. She was wearing another of those dratted nightgowns that only packaged her up like the most succulent gift.

He longed to taste her.

"Cecily," he murmured.

"Are you drunk?"

"Mm." The temptation to laugh overwhelmed him. Sober, he most certainly would not have been here. And yet here he was. "Do you object, wife of mine?"

"You haven't visited my bedchamber in—" She broke off, as though recalling precisely how long it had been.

He could have counted the minutes.

"An excruciatingly long time," he said.

Her eyes met his, almost fearless. Perhaps even curious. Intrigued. There was no fear there, though he thought he caught the hint of uncertainty. This was not how they usually were.

Then again, how they usually were had broken his heart more times than he could ever have said.

She stared up at him as though she expected him to take her any second, pressing her into the mattress with the weight of his body, opening her legs with his hips so he could settle between them. Where he belonged.

For perhaps the first time, she did not look as though she would mind.

"Percy," she said. A question, an invitation.

For a moment, he could not think of anything but the extent of his want for her. Drugging, intoxicating, demanding. If he chose it, perhaps tonight she would allow to him take all the things she'd denied him for so long, and tomorrow he could nurse his hangover and the fractures of his broken heart.

Tempting, but he was not that drunk.

There would always be a tomorrow. If he gave himself to her now, he did not think he could face the tomorrow she would offer them.

"I'm sorry for waking you," he said, clumsier than usual as he pushed himself back and to his feet. Thankfully, it was not far until he reached his own room—or else he might never have made it. "Sleep well, Cecy."

The nickname slipped from his lips unintentionally. A remnant of the past crashing into their present. It had been a long time since he had given her an endearment; she'd always told him how much she hated that name.

And yet now, she merely stared at him as though waiting for something that would make sense of this interaction.

He, too, was waiting.

"Goodnight," he said, the words slurring a little as he walked in an almost straight line across her room once more. Some small part of him regretted passing over what had essentially been the most enthusiastic consent he had received in years, but he had too much respect for himself to give way to this.

If he was to have her, he would have all of her, or he would have none at all.

"Percy," she said when he reached the doorway. "Where were you tonight?"

"White's. As I told you."

The silence that greeted him made him feel as though he had somehow said the wrong thing, although he'd only given her the truth.

All their marriage, aside from that lamentable oversight with Caroline, he had given her his truth.

"You didn't visit her?" she asked finally.

He turned to find Cecily watching him, the moonlight washing her in ghostly light. She could have been a wraith, only half real. Sometimes he felt that way himself.

"No." This word was stronger than his others, more certain. "I didn't."

She slid down the pillows, drawing the blankets up over her head. "You'll have a sore head in the morning," was all she said. And yet, as Percy fell face-first into bed, not so much as bothering to ring for his valet, he felt as though that day, and accompanying night, had done more for their marriage than all the wooing of the past four years.

Chapter Five

Percy awoke with a very bad head. A reminder once again that he should not be indulging as freely as he had done twenty years ago. Back then, he might have emerged at least reasonably functional. As it was, by eleven, he had barely allowed the blinds to be drawn and daylight to enter the room—and even that made his head throb.

A knock sounded at the door. "Enter," he called, fully expecting the breakfast he'd asked to be delivered to his room. Instead, Cecily poked her auburn head through, a tray in her hands.

"You asked for this to be sent," she said, not meeting his gaze as she brought it to a table in the corner and set it carefully down. "I also took the liberty of asking them to make you some coffee. Mama always used to have some in the mornings when she indulged."

His stomach flipped at the reminder that she, evidently, recalled his transgression the previous evening. Any equilibrium he'd hoped to find promptly disappeared.

"This is unexpected," he said, forcing himself out of bed. His robe lay discarded on the back of a chair and he wrapped it firmly around his waist. His head pounded, and if they were to engage in any verbal sparring, he hoped she would at least save it for after they had eaten. "I hadn't realised I'd requested you to be the one to bring me my meals."

"I thought you might be suffering."

He made a noise at the back of his head, biting back his wince as he sank into the chair at the spindly table. On occasion, he wrote his letters here, and her gaze flicked to the pot of ink that sat ready.

To his surprise, he enjoyed the first sip of coffee, and he thought perhaps the day might not be utterly intolerable. "Did your mother often overindulge?"

"Sometimes." Cecily shrugged and hovered behind another chair. For the first time, he noticed a letter in her hand. "She wrote to me again last week."

"Oh?" He took another sip and allowed himself a corner of dry toast.

"She's asking about . . ." Cecily sucked in a breath, and her cheeks turned red. Percy frowned at the expression, realising for the first time that she had not come merely out of solicitude. To fortify himself, he took a larger bite, and considered the pound cake and muffins, wondering if he could stomach them.

"Asking about what?"

"She's asking about children," she said in a rush. "Our children, to be exact. And . . ."

Percy knew the answer as well as she did. There could be no chance of children from an empty bed. And although he had come dangerously close to sharing that bed with her last night, he had not succumbed, and their marriage remained unconsummated.

He nodded at the paper in her hands. "Is that the letter?"

"Yes."

"May I see?"

Reluctantly, she handed it over, and he scanned the pages. As always, the viscountess wrote with an impertinent that infuriated him, demanding to know why there had been no issue from their marriage, and whether Cecily had the bad luck to be barren.

"How discourteous," he said lightly, dropping the letter back onto the tray.

"Would you . . ." She glanced up at him hesitantly. "Would you help me form a reply?"

"Certainly. Phrasing or content?" A rare flash of anger passed through him. When he'd married her, one of his many reasons had been to separate her from the woman who'd always treated her with borderline cruelty. "Or better still, don't reply at all."

"You'd have me ignore my own mother?"

"She's been little enough involved until she thought you might have a child she could get her claws into." He knew his words were uncharitable, but he couldn't quite hold them back. For years, he'd kept his opinions about her mother, even about William, to himself, but he found his self-control lacking in the face of his monstrous hangover.

This would be the last time he drank so heavily. He should have known better.

"I do not care to have my wife bullied," he said, finally.

"I thought you had no wish for me to be your wife any longer."

His laugh was short and a little bitter, but when he took her hand in his, long fingers enclosing around her smaller ones, she didn't pull away. "Perhaps I'm tired of being denied," he murmured. "And it is easier not to try. But no matter what we might wish, some things do not change."

"Do you regret marrying me?" she blurted.

His fingers tightened, and his gaze dropped to them. "What a troublesome question. I have no easy answer for you."

She looked almost disappointed, as though she'd been hoping for an answer in the negative—but how could he say he didn't regret marrying her when she went out of her way to inspire that regret every day? *She* certainly regretted their union, and he was tired of pretending.

"People will start to talk if I continue to be without child."

Was she suggesting what it sounded like she was suggesting? He dropped her hand. "Let them."

"My mother will—"

"Your mother will not find herself welcome in my house if she comes to interfere."

"You didn't seem to mind her interference when you arranged with her to marry me."

"And if I could have done so from your word alone, I would have, allow me to reassure you of that." He searched her face, seeing only confusion there, and perhaps even hurt. This was not how he'd imagined this conversation going. "I never meant to hurt you, Cecily. If there had been another way—but that boy tried to ruin you. People saw you leave the ballroom together. What else could I have done?"

He saw the moment his words registered. Her eyes widened and she rose from her chair. "Perhaps you could have allowed him to marry me himself," she said, her voice choked.

This delusion was insufferable. Percy replaced his cup on the saucer with more force than he intended. "Is that what you truly think?"

"He loved me!"

"He thought you were easy prey. And my goodness, Cecily, was he wrong?"

She blanched, and he immediately regretted his words. Still, better she knew now. Better he take what remained of her love for this man—one that had never existed outside her mind—and squashed it. And if he condemned any chance he had of winning her back, then so be it. The chance of that had never been high in the first place; that was not why he had attempted to distance himself from her.

"Let me be plain, Cecily, seeing as you have been labouring under a misapprehension over the course of our time together. William Devereaux had no intentions of marrying you. He would have ruined you as he has ruined many other young ladies, and your chances of a good marriage would have been materially diminished. If you had loved him and he intended to do the honourable thing, I would never have interfered, believe me. I'm not as cruel as you believe me to be. But he has never loved you, my songbird. And he certainly would never have married you."

"I—" Cecily shook her head. "You can't know that."

He dragged his hands through his hair, head throbbing and his stomach turning. "Of course I know that. It's hardly a secret what William Devereaux is. There's a reason no mother worth her salt will allow him access to her daughters. He's barred from every reputable club, and I doubt he will secure many invitations now he's returned to London." He waited for the shock to cross her face at that particular revelation, but as she just looked at him with wide eyes, he snorted. "No doubt you also knew that, too. Have you met him since his return? Has he renewed his addresses?"

She swallowed, all the confirmation he could have needed. Abruptly tired and in need of more coffee, he sank back into his seat. "No matter. I tried to save you once, and it made a fool of me." He massaged his temples. "What would you like to say to your mother?"

Her gaze fell to the letter still in her hands, then up at him. Her eyes were wet, and he sighed at the knowledge he had likely broken her heart with another man's betrayal.

"I'm sorry," he said, more gently this time, and picked up her hand, pressing it to his lips in a chaste kiss. "I should not have lost my temper with you."

"No, I . . ." Her voice came out scratchy and weak. "Is that truly what you believe? That he cared nothing for me?"

Though this realisation was one he'd been hoping she would come to for four years now, he took no pleasure in his answer. "No more than his other conquests. If I thought he had honest intentions, I would have allowed matters to play out as they would." He released her hand. "Do you believe me?"

She released a shaky breath. "I don't know. I wish . . ." *Things had been different*, he could almost hear her say.

"As do I," he said heavily, and turned his attention back to his breakfast. "Thank you for the coffee, Cecily. It's much appreciated. If you need me to help draft a letter to your mother, you may find me at any time."

Understanding the dismissal, she rose, brushing out her skirts. After a hesitation, in which he was certain she would say something, she left him to his breakfast and the reflection that at least now, if she intended to take William as a lover, she would do so in the full knowledge of everything he was.

At first, Cecily had been determined to reject Percy's assertion. After all, what would he know about the subject? But when she invited Arabella to join her for afternoon tea, she discovered confirmation in the worst of places: from her very best friend.

"Oh, of course he isn't an honourable man," Arabella said, swallowing a large mouthful of plum cake. "Dearest, do you truly think a man capable of flirting with *such* skill to be one who has never made a fool of a woman before?"

Cecily stared at her teacup. "Well, I did think he loved me."

"If only we'd known each other better back then." Arabella sighed. "Even I could have told you. Everyone knew he was a rake. Well, according to everything I've heard, he still *is* a rake. I imagine he just wanted to kiss you. Or worse, of course, but your father *was* a viscount, so perhaps he hadn't intended to strip you of your virtue. Not while you were unmarried, at least." She cut herself another slice of cake, oblivious to the way Cecily's stomach twisted and dropped.

"Do you think he would have married me if we were discovered?" Cecily asked. "I mean—"

"You *were* discovered. I thought you said Percy discovered you both."

Cecily recalled the way Percy had taken William's lapels, pulled him up, and delivered such a devastating blow that she feared William's nose had broken. Certainly, there had been plenty of blood. And William, instead of swearing his honour, had fled.

Percy had been the one to guide her back to the house, apologising for the violence even as he wiped his bloodied knuckles and led her to a side door so she could rejoin the party and her mother. He had assured her that she would be all right, and she had been so shaken by the entire situation that she had—

Well, she had believed him, and her naïve heart had hoped that the form of 'all right' would be William declaring that he wished to marry her. Instead, Percy had been the one to come forward, and she'd been able to do nothing but accept with William gone.

For the first time, anger at William stirred in her chest. *He* had been the one to flee, the one to take her outside and kiss her and then say nothing about marriage. All this time, she had assumed that had they *not* been discovered, he would have married her, but surely it should have been the other way around. They *had* been discovered, and the honourable thing would have been to offer for her immediately.

"Heavens," she said faintly. "I have been a fool."

Arabella patted her hand sympathetically. "We are all fools at nineteen."

"I am a fool *now*. He invited me to the Pantheon for a masquerade."

"Perhaps he thought he could seduce you," Arabella said with a shrug. "I'll admit, I thought you would be amenable to the idea. I never assumed that you . . ."

"I wanted to *marry* him!"

"Yes, well." Her friend wrinkled her nose. "I didn't think you had such appalling judgement, dearest."

Cecily scowled. Four years of her life pining for a man who had never harboured honest intentions towards her. Four years of being furious at Percy for ruining her chances of happiness when he had, in fact, been attempting to save her.

How mortifying.

"I thought I could love him," she said. "That my life would have been perfect if Percy had never found us. What a *fool* I've been. And now William thinks he can win me over again with a few compliments?"

"He almost did," Arabella pointed out.

"Unhelpful, Bella."

"What will you do now?"

Heavens, wasn't that a thought. She frowned, worrying on her lower lip. First, she had an apology to make, and then . . . Well, she supposed *then* she would decide what to do about the masquerade.

It was not until a mere few hours before the masquerade that Cecily encountered Percy again in their dressing room. He looked as though he intended to leave without speaking, and she hurried to him, putting a hand on his arm.

"Will you give me a moment of your time?"

"Cecily." He glanced down at her, a pinch between his brows. "Do you need something?"

"I told my mother to stop asking so many questions about our intimate life," she said, feeling the slightest glow of pride at the way a slow smile spread across his face.

"Did you indeed? Good. And if she persists, allow me to write to her instead."

"You hardly have to ask my permission."

"I'd prefer to have your consent."

He always did.

Even when drunk, he had stopped before anything could have happened between them. Cecily couldn't help wondering, in the final moments before sleep, what might have happened if he had given into his natural marital impulses. After all, he *was* her husband and she his wife. And she believed him when he said he had not been with Caroline.

When Arabella had spoken about love, she had always mentioned it coming from the heart. Yet after that night, whenever Cecily looked at Percy, it was her stomach that twisted and fluttered and dropped.

Disgust, she told herself.

She could no longer delude herself into believing it was true.

"I did meet William," she blurted, seeing the surprise cross Percy's face. His frown deepened.

"And?"

"You are *certain* he would not have married me?"

"As far as any man could be."

The hurt that she'd once felt at the betrayal now just felt like a lump in the base of her stomach. Time truly had worn away the depth of her feelings, and the shallow inclination she felt towards him now was easily overwhelmed by the force of her anger.

"Then," she said, summoning her courage, "I suppose I ought to apologise."

"An apology?" Percy's brows rose, but he gave the barest hint of a smile. "For what, pray?"

"I thought you married me for selfish reasons."

He observed her gravely. "Why, my songbird, I did. Yes, in doing so I protected you from other such men, and the machinations of your mother, but I would not have done that if I were not very much in love with you."

Her stomach flipped with such force that she almost gasped. Such simple words, and he had certainly said things like this to her before, but oddly it had never felt like *this.*

She tucked her shaking hands behind her back so he would not see her nervousness. "The masquerade is tonight," she said, looking up at him. His gaze was intent on her mouth, as though he could read the words on the tip of her tongue. "Do you have plans?"

His eyes flicked from her mouth to her eyes, the frown in them more pronounced than ever, and disappointment crashed through her even before he spoke. "I do," he said slowly, and her newfound confidence crumbled.

"Oh." Like a coward, she retreated for her bedchamber door. "Well, then. I suppose I should begin to get ready. Goodnight, Percy. I hope you have fun."

"I have no doubt I will," he murmured as she fled for the relative safety of her bedchamber. To her relief, when her maid arrived several minutes later to dress her for the evening, she mentioned nothing about the redness of Cecily's eyes.

Chapter Six

The Pantheon blazed with candlelight, laughter, and the sweep of strings. Cecily entered on William Devereaux's arm, all her suspicions coming true. He was indeed a flirt of magnificent levels, and he exuded arrogant confidence, no doubt that she would fall for his charms.

One could perfume excrement, but that did not make it taste any better. Even so, the magnificence of the building replaced her thoughts of discontent with ones of wonder.

Everything was so very *golden.* Lights reflected from gilt vases, adding to the illusion of gold. If she tilted her head back, she could make out the famous stuccos—grotesque, but oddly charming, in a distinctly gothic style. A dome rose overhead, and even the walls of the ballrooms were lusciously painted. Guests milled around statues of the Roman gods and goddesses.

If Cecily had been there alone—and a more dangerous thing for a lady she could not conceive—she would have been content to stare all day at its grandeur.

Unfortunately, she was not alone.

To his credit, William behaved very charmingly for the first two dances, all outrageous compliments and very few wandering hands or eyes. He boasted about his experiences in Italy and the magnificence of the architecture there, and if Cecily hadn't noticed the dangerous gleam in his eye, she might have thought the outing an innocent one.

That was, until he led her to a darkened corner, one hand to the small of her back, and when she twisted away, he caught her arm.

If she had ever needed confirmation he was not who she had once thought him to be, this was it.

"Come now, petal," he said, gripping her a little too strongly. "I know you've missed me. Wearing the willow for me all these years."

She turned to look at him. "Is that what you think? I'm married now, William."

"Ah yes, to that stuffy baronet. Does he keep you locked up, my flower? Did you have to escape his clutches to come here with me? Never fear—I shall contrive ways for you to escape his reach. When I want something, I am not denied."

A bead of sweat rolled down her spine. Even if she had been in a mood to partake in an assignation, the heat would have been enough to put her off. Nothing was less appealing than feeling damp and uncomfortable. Not one gentleman considered that when they made their advances in the bitter cold or the height of summer.

And with all the bodies crammed in around them? The multitudes of candles that lit the place?

Yes, it looked all very romantic, and she would brave the heat to dance, but decidedly *not* for this.

He pressed still closer, forcing her to attempt to step back—and encounter a wall. Really, was he going to force himself on her in public? Instead of fear, she only felt a burst of anger. Perhaps he thought she hadn't grown since the age of nineteen, when she had been so desperate for his affection, but he would shortly find that wasn't the case.

Still, she had come here with him to find the truth once and for all.

"I have a question for you," she said, staring into his handsome face and wondering how she could have been so deceived by it. "If we had not been discovered all those years ago, what would you have done?"

A grin spread slowly across his face. "Perhaps we could find out here, petal."

"Perhaps not. Would you have married me?"

"What does that matter now? You married another."

"Because you *fled* when he discovered us."

His grip on her arm tightened once more. "What else was I to do when he revealed he had bought my debts and would call them in if I didn't leave the country at once?" he growled. "Four years I stayed away, all because of him."

Cecily suffered three unpleasant shocks in one. The first was that Percy, in all in his gallant efforts to protect her, had sent William away, and *that* was why he had left the country.

The second was that William no doubt saw seducing her as a form of revenge. Once again, his actions had no bearing on his feelings for her as a woman.

The third was that, then and now, she was an idiot.

"But," William said, his tone once again smooth and charming, "we need not concern ourselves with that."

She shoved him back. "At which point did you think I would forsake my marriage vows for the sake of a man whom I have not seen for four years?" she asked icily. "One whom, moreover, tried to ruin me?"

"You did well for yourself out of it. Married your rich baronet and lived the life of luxury. Really, you ought to be thanking me for forcing his hand. Maybe he would never have offered for you otherwise." William's breath was hot against her cheek as he leant in, pressing her more firmly against the wall. "And now we are free to have our fun together with no fear of ruin or repercussions. Is that not something?"

"This is *not* my idea of fun."

"It will be once I've kissed you."

Although Cecily had hoped William had grown out of being the scoundrel he had once been, she had not come unprepared. Her maid, at her request, had pinned her hair up with several large hairpins, one of which she withdrew now, jamming it into the fleshy part of his arm. He howled and leapt back, colliding with the wall and almost sliding behind the curtains. A few masked guests looked around, but the purpose of a masquerade was not so they could become involved with another's business, and they quickly turned away again.

"Do *not* think you can touch me without my permission," she said with all the cold dignity she could muster. "Or you may be certain I'll do that again."

"What the *devil* was that for?" he hissed, clutching his arm. It was bleeding, she noted dispassionately. "You've ruined my best coat!"

"Well, then. Next time, I hope you'll accept a lady's refusal when she gives it." Cecily turned and surveyed the crowd, keeping her head high as she located her second mistake of the evening.

Stabbing her only method of returning home.

If she had fully thought this through, she would have procured an alternate method of travelling home. William's ego would not take her besting him lightly, and he was definitely not enough of a gentleman to escort her back home. At least, not without her relinquishing something in return.

Not for the first time, she wished Percy had been available to escort her instead. With him, she could be safe, at liberty to enjoy the dancing and the thrill without fear. Her lip quivered, and she tilted her chin up higher.

A figure emerged from the gloom beside her, and she started, thinking for a moment it was William. But no: this figure was far taller and broader, and instead of wearing a black mask as William had done, his was white and feathered, just like hers. Her gaze dropped to his hands, and she frowned. They looked familiar—ones she had seen around a book recently; ones that she had imagined pressed against her skin.

"Bravo," Percy said, nodding to William. "A truly magnificent performance."

There could be no mistaking it. Percy was *here*. Percy, her husband, whom she had *distinctly* heard saying had an engagement tonight. Could he have meant this? Or did he arrive because he thought she wanted him to?

The question was, did he recognise her?

The spark in his eyes told her that he did. And he was waiting to take his lead from her—whether she confessed to recognising him, or whether they would continue as strangers.

The thought appealed. No history between them, no resentment, none of the difficulties that had plagued their marriage since its outset. If she could pretend she did not know him, would she like him?

So she tilted her head and smiled. "I like to think I am not a lady to be trifled with."

"I would be tempted to agree."

"I don't suppose you would like to dance?"

He stepped a little closer, the difference in height between them so achingly familiar. "Would you?"

"Yes. You see, unfortunately my former partner is indisposed."

Percy turned his amused glance after William, who was storming away through the crowd. A lady in a provocative dress attempted to stand in his way, fluttering her fan at him, but he shoved her aside. A surprise, given his tastes, but clearly he was in a rage.

"I cannot think it too much of a shame," he said. "Your former partner does not strike me as an agreeable gentleman."

"He was not," she said with feeling, casting another glance at Percy, certain he had seen the whole sorry affair and knew precisely who William was.

"Then may I say how relieved I am to hear you are no longer in his clutches."

"I have not been for a while."

He eyed her thoughtfully, then smiled. "I'm glad to hear it." He held out his hand to her. "Your dance, ma'am."

She accepted his hand and allowed him to lead her into the middle of the floor. A Viennese waltz was playing, and she felt a little flutter of nerves as he laid his hand on her waist. "My hairpin is very accessible," she warned him.

He chuckled, low under his breath. "I doubt anyone who saw you in action would ever consider you an easy target, my dear."

"May I have a name to call you by?"

His hesitation was so slight, she barely felt it, and then he nodded, leaning in a little closer. "Why not Odysseus? You could be Circe."

"Circe?" She raised her brows. "Are you afraid I might turn you into a pig?"

"Not in the slightest," he said, amused again. "If you recall, his men were the ones turned into pigs—she did not manage to trick *him*."

"What are you trying to insinuate?"

"They were in love for a year before their parting," he murmured. "Once she had lifted the enchantment over his men."

Her stomach clenched and dipped, and the hand he held in hers trembled slightly. She struggled to retain her composure.

Why *now* she should be so affected by his profession of love, even in this lighthearted way, she didn't know.

And yet.

And *yet.*

She gave him her best teasing smile. "I'm afraid I don't have a year to spare you."

"No?" He leaned ever closer, his cheek brushing against the side of her mask as he delivered his words straight into her ear. "How about a night?"

She shivered. The whole proposition felt entirely sordid, even if it *was* her husband. Still, she fancied William was watching, and she decided it would not hurt to allow herself this one liberty. She allowed herself to melt into Percy's arms. "Perhaps a night." Her voice sounded nothing like her usual self—it was deep, husky, a throaty hum that made his eyes spark. "But a night is not enough to fall in love."

"Is it not? Tell that to my heart, which has been yours since I saw you stab that man so masterfully."

"Have you always been attracted to violence?"

"Only when it comes in the form of hairpins." He twirled her slowly, one hand grazing her waist. The other grasped hers. Their bodies were not close, not particularly, but despite the overpowering warmth in the air, she felt the heat from his chest.

She could not see the colour in his eyes, but she knew it anyway. Four years of reluctant marriage had taught her that his eyes were mingled brown and green, lighter when he looked at her, and sometimes darker.

His palm skimmed her waist, and she wondered if his eyes were dark now.

In truth, she hungered for it.

There was nothing ladylike or pure about her wants and desires; it was as though he had unlocked something inside her by those almost moments, the anticipation that never came to fruition.

The tender flesh between her legs throbbed at the soft press of his hand against the small of her back, and she thought it entirely possible she had gone mad.

To punish him for making her want him, she cocked her head and gave him a saucy smile. "You should know I'm married."

He gave an answering smile, roguish in a way she was *certain* she had not seen before. Surely she would have noticed her husband being *roguish.* "Not to that unsavoury gentleman, I hope?"

"Oh no." She tittered a laugh. "Very much not. He was nothing. An idle flirtation, long ended."

"Is *that* so?" His voice deepened to a seductive rumble she'd never heard directed at her. "Tell me, Circe, is that all I am to you?"

"What else could you expect to be? We only have one night."

"True." His fingers grazed up her spine. "Then I suppose we should make it count."

For a few moments, they danced in silence. Cecily could remember nothing of the world around them; the only thing that anchored her in place was the steady weight of his eyes, and the surety of his hands.

Eventually, she could bear the silence no more, and looked at the shape of his mouth, just visible from underneath his mask. "What of you?" she asked. "Do you have a wife?"

Amusement radiated through him at her question, but he kept to the unspoken game they were playing. "I do."

"And yet you are here, flirting with strange ladies."

"Mm." The hand on her back moved to her side and gripped her hip, just for an instant. A heartbeat later, he was holding her as properly as a saint, but the squeeze had been so familiar, so possessive, that her head spun. "I do not think you are so strange to me, my witch."

She took a moment to regain her bearings. "I fear you must make for a poor husband."

"Perhaps. But you overestimate the investment of my wife."

Her pulse quickened. "I doubt that."

"At best, she is indifferent to me."

She did not feel indifferent now. If anything, her skin felt more sensitive than ever, chafing under her clothes until she longed to rip them free of her body. The heat that rose in her coiled in her lower belly, and she could not blame her flush on the stuffiness of the air.

"I hardly think that likely," she said, feeling as though she was gasping for air.

His hand slid up her spine again, flattening across her shoulder blades as though he intended to pull her against him, before thinking better of it. She longed for that pressure, even as his fingers made their infuriatingly slow path back down her spine.

Then lower, just above the swell of her buttocks. In plain view of the other masked guests. Testing her limits.

Cecily's breath caught, but she refused to pull away. If this was a game of whose will would break first, she would not succumb. After all, as improper as this might be, they were at a masquerade, and he was her husband. Of all the men on earth, the only one who had the right to lay hands on her—if she permitted it.

And permit it she did as his fingers explored the soft silk of her dress. Almost venturing low enough to be indecent, but never quite. His eyes hypnotised her, unnervingly beautiful in the dim light.

How could she ever have thought him old?

His head descended still lower, a fraction of a thought away from hers. It would be the work of a moment to tilt her face and catch his mouth against her own. A kiss. Her blood burned for it, pounded in her veins, demanding she take. For once in their marriage, all she wanted was him.

"Tell me one reason I should believe that my wife has any investment whatsoever in my exploits?" he murmured, breath brushing the damp skin of her lower lip. "Give me a reason to believe my wife cares about my comings and goings."

Cecily's fingers dug convulsively into his shoulders. "All wives care."

"Is that so?" The question shivered across her skin.

"All those that I know, at least."

"Even ones that never wished to marry their husband in the first place?"

Her heart hammered against her ribs, but they were in too deep for her to do anything but give him her truth. "Even then."

"Mm." He pulled her even closer. They'd spiralled out to the very edge of the dancing crowd, beside a pillar and bronze vase. Although people surrounded them on all sides, she felt as though they were invisible, alone in a world that only held the two of them. "You surprise me."

"Ladies are taught not to expect fidelity from one's husband, but I don't think that stops us from wanting it."

"Oh?" His knuckles brushed the line of her jaw. "And who might have told you that, my witch?"

"My mother made my role as a wife plain when I married."

A noise rumbled in his chest that sounded distinctly like displeasure. "It strikes me that perhaps she might not know all there is to know about happiness in marriage."

"She was married for a great many years before my father died."

"Perhaps she was." He backed her against a pillar, the cool marble leeching through the thin material of her dress and chemise. His hand came to her waist, sitting at its curve as though it was made to fit the shape of her body. "But does that mean she knows what is best for you and your marriage?" His nose nudged her earlobe, and her breath stuttered. "You are not your mother, and your husband is not your father. Do not tar us all with the same brush. We are not *all* unfaithful."

Her father had been. Even as a girl, she had known that, hiding in the library as her mother had thrown ornaments at the wall over rumours of her father attending the opera with his mistress. Over the accounts proving he'd housed the very same mistress in an exclusive location in London.

"Is that to say you have never once strayed over the course of your marriage?"

He turned his head, and she thought she heard him inhale. "Not once."

"I find that hard to believe."

"Do you? I made vows, sweet Circe. I swore them to my wife and to my family and to God, and I have no intention of betraying them."

If they had still been dancing, she would have stopped. As it was, the cool of the pillar against her back and the warmth of his body against her front, all she could do was tilt her head back to look at him. "You recall your vows?"

"Do you not?"

She did—she recalled the day as clear as if it were cut from crystal. The small church, the handful of people there to celebrate a marriage she had never asked for, and a husband standing in all his finery, swearing to love her, comfort her, honour and keep her.

She, in turn, had agreed to obey, serve, honour and keep him. And when she had looked into his eyes, she had seen only sincerity.

It had terrified her.

"We agreed to forsake all other," she said.

"Yes."

And yet they were here, with each other but not, pretending to live a lie because it was easier than admitting the truth.

She rested her hand lightly on his shoulder. "It seems we are both liars," she whispered.

His arm slid further around her waist, pressing her against him. Not flush, but enough that her breasts brushed his chest. At the contact, her nipples hardened. Her face heated, and she prayed he couldn't feel or see, even if the sensitivity fluttered through her body like lazy butterflies.

She was a flower slowly coming awake, and he was the sun.

Tonight, she would allow herself to feel.

Slowly, he brought their clasped hands to his mouth and kissed her knuckles. His mouth was hot against her skin. When he spoke, his voice had lowered. "Dance with me."

Chapter Seven

It did not feel like dancing at all, the way they moved and came back together. Percy wondered if it was the most united they had been since the day in that tiny, stifling church, sunlight spiralling through the air. When he urged her closer, she obeyed, head tilting back to bare her elegant neck. Her eyes locked on his, unmoving, hot and heavy in the candlelight.

Time and reality parted to give way to this moment, the music swelling and his hands on her body the way she had never allowed when they were not pretending.

Tomorrow—but he could not think of tomorrow. There was only tonight.

Her lips tempted him, lush and full beneath the white feathers of her mask. Her hair, tightly coiled and pinned to the back of her head, gleamed like sunlit autumn leaves. Coming here had been a spur-of-the-moment decision, one made before he had even known what he was doing. After she had accepted his judgement of William, he'd given himself leave to hope, and when he had seen her rejection of William's advances, he couldn't have stayed away even if he'd wanted to.

And he had not, in that moment, wanted to.

Now, he could not bring himself to regret it; he felt the arousal in her body as surely as he did in his. Here, playing at being strangers, there was no need to hide behind the mask of familiarity and the way things had been between them.

They ate, they drank, and they danced. The night deepened and eventually sunrise harkened the onset of morning. The candles guttered, replaced by servants carrying new ones. Guests napped on sofas, or withdrew to nooks and corners, or perhaps unoccupied rooms, unwilling for the night to end. The ballroom emptied, fellow dancers leaving with each new set.

Still they moved together, hands clasping, bodies twisting and moving, parting always to come back together again. Each reunion, as brief as it was, sent relief coursing through his body. Though he'd deliberately not had anything to drink that evening, he felt intoxicated. Inebriated. Out of his senses.

"Odysseus," she said, breaking the silence between them. "Epic hero. Is that not an audacious claim?"

Percy twisted her into a darkened corner, not missing a step even as his thumb smoothed over the bare skin of her hand. They turned, and a shudder ran through her. She pressed up against him, trapping him against the wall, and he wondered if the act were consciously done. He doubted it.

"He was perhaps a bad hero to choose, in retrospect," he said.

"Why? Because he went on many adventures?" she teased him, leaning in, her eyes hypnotic. "Or perhaps because he was daring and bold."

"Because he did not love his wife as much as he claimed to."

"You don't think he loved her? Legend says he did."

"Legend has a habit of distorting the truth."

"Well, he *claimed* to love her, then. I think he believed he did."

He placed his hand on her waist, knowing no one was watching, and not particularly caring if they did. His thumb pressed against her ribcage, inches from the underside of her breast. She was such a slight thing, so easily breakable. Yet, for all that, she had broken him more times than he ever could, and with a far lighter touch. "Is that the same?" he murmured.

"For some men, it is."

"You have a poor opinion of mankind." He swiped his thumb up higher, and her breath caught. "Are we so very irredeemable?"

Her eyelids fluttered as though she heard the silent question underneath his voiced one. *Am I so irredeemable*?

"I thought—perhaps—so." Her fingers gripped his coat, ensuring he could not escape even if he had wanted to. "Now I hardly know what to think."

His back brushed the wall, and he tightened his hold on her, drawing her flush against his body for the first time. The feel of the contact made him want to groan, to whisper her name and unpin her hair so it fell over her shoulders the way it had the previous night in her bed.

Yet the moment he did, their game would be at an end. Once he undid their pretence, he would not be able to stitch it into being once again.

He was not sure if he would want to.

She leant back, gazing into his face. Her hand rose, fingers brushing the edges of his mask. An indifferent disguise, as ineffectual as hers. "I do not wish to think about tomorrow," she whispered.

He caught her wrist, fingers gentle, and brought it to his mouth. Soft, so soft, under his mouth, the scent of her perfume more pronounced here. Hardly breathing, she allowed the caress.

"Then let us live in denial a little longer," he whispered, and when he flicked his tongue across the line of her vein, she gasped. "Allow me one thing, sweet Circe."

"What is that?"

"Allow me to kiss you."

The shadows of reality beckoned as she watched him. "Why?"

"Because I have wanted to since first I saw you." He drew her arm over his shoulder and played his winning card. "We only have one night."

Consequences. The word thudded dully at the back of his mind, and he knew it played in her mind, too. However much they didn't want to face up to what this meant, tomorrow they must. A conversation was in order.

But for tonight . . . Tonight they could play at falling in love and nothing more.

She leant against him, eyes widening as she encountered his erection pressing against her stomach. Even if he had wanted to deny wanting her, this rendered it impossible.

He didn't mind. Let her know. If she had been paying attention over the course of their marriage, it would be nothing new. An old reality, no longer shocking.

Still, what looked like surprise flitted across her eyes, and her breath came in a short spurt.

He ached.

His thumb brushed the underside of her breast.

Both hands braced on his shoulders, she rose onto her tiptoes, rubbing up against him with innocent sensuality as she brought her mouth against his.

Allow me to kiss you, he had said. Expecting, as had always been the case, to be the one to initiate. He had expected that she would yield, and perhaps—as he hoped—enjoy what pleasure it brought her. Instead, she wrapped her arms around his neck and held herself in place as she kissed him. Clumsily at first, their lips unaccustomed to the feel of the other's. Unaccustomed to the sensation of her taking control.

Percy yielded. Both hands moved to her waist to support her as he returned her kiss gently, not letting her feel the way her tongue sent need rampaging through him. When she nipped at his bottom lip, he tightened his hold on her, stifling the groan. But by the way her lips curved in a smile, she understood what lay behind his restraint.

If he had his way, he would lay her bare and find a surface to take her against. Any would do. The wall, even, if she would permit him spreading her legs and pushing between them.

He blinked back all the lurid fantasies that sprung to mind, knowing he could never give way to them here. Or, perhaps, anywhere, if she refused to allow her body its desires. For as long as they had been married, she'd locked up the moment her body had responded to him. Out of resentment, he was sure. A feeling of loyalty, in some twisted way, to the man she had believed herself to love.

And so he held himself still as she tilted her head, finding the place their mouths slotted together as though they were made for one another. Her tongue slid against his, gently probing and gaining in confidence at the shiver that rocked through him. His hips jerked, out of control, seeking friction against her. In response, a moan tore from her throat, and she clung to him more tightly.

His restraint slipped, just for a second, and he felt around her to grip her backside. Such perfect curves, lush and soft in all the right places. He'd never known want until it came with red hair and green eyes and lips that were as wont to pout as smile.

He throbbed for her, kissing her back more urgently, showing her with his mouth all the things he longed to do elsewhere. Taste her. Lick her. Find her pleasure and bring about her climax the way she had never allowed him—but tonight, he knew, the usual rules did not apply, and she would give him all the things she had denied their entire marriage. Not merely sex, but *desire.*

And where would that leave them?

Gasping, she broke away, staring up at him through the shadows with wide, lustful eyes and swollen lips. "There," she said, voice throaty in a way that made him burn. "Your kiss, sir."

She had no inkling, no real idea, what she did to him.

He turned her, now being the one to press her against the wall with the weight of his body. He waited for her to move, but she kept still, breathless the way she had been that night in her bed. Waiting.

But the day closed in, dawn light filtering through the windows, the dome. The night was at an end.

As he met her gaze, he expected her to pull away, to hide behind the walls she'd erected before they'd even married. Instead, she met him with an expression so fierce, it should not have been so lovely.

Perhaps instead of Circe, his enchantress, he should have named her Boudicca.

"It's almost time," he said, pressing a kiss to her forehead. "My night is at an end."

She closed her eyes, nostrils flaring. "We only promised each other one night." It sounded almost like a curse.

"We did." He stepped back and bowed. "Allow me to take you home."

For a moment, he thought she might ask for something else—something more. Instead, she nodded slowly. "Keep your mask on," she said, and he understood her meaning. *Keep pretending.*

"Of course. Tonight, I am nothing but a hero of legend."

The smile didn't reach her eyes. "A philanderer."

"Now *that* I cannot agree with." He touched her chin with the tip of one finger, and her eyes met his, open and searching, the fierceness fading into vulnerability that made his heart ache. "Not all legends are true, sweet Circe."

She took hold of his wrist and brought his fingers to her lips. A gesture that she had never bestowed upon him before. But when she looked up again, all he could see was resignation across her face. "Call your carriage. I think it's time for us to leave."

Cecily kept silent on the carriage ride home. Their pretence was unravelling, thread by thread, with every yard they travelled. All she had were questions.

Had it always been like this with Percy?

Back when he had first started to court her, she couldn't remember it ever feeling like *this*. Butterflies and flirtations and . . .

They'd talked. Of course they had, when they'd first met. He'd been a friend to her, and music had drawn them together—and even then, she had loved the duets they sang, as though time paused whenever his voice joined hers, and her heart ached, and she felt that wanting inside herself for *more*. But once the song ended, she had gone back to pining over William and thinking of Percy as a friend. A father figure, almost, showing interest in her because he wanted to encourage her interests, not because he was in love with her.

Now she wondered if she had ever known what love was. Being with Percy did not make her heart yearn with the same desperate intensity as it had with William when she was nineteen. He was not a firework but the steady burn of a coal fire, all embers and occasional flame.

And she had kissed him.

The memory of it brought a hot flush to her cheeks. An ache between her legs that she didn't remember feeling before. Vainly, she rubbed her thighs together, only stopping when he glanced down at the movement. If anything, that only made the aching worse.

She'd never wanted like this before. And especially not *Percy*. Silver-haired, patient-eyed Percy, who had spurned her not hours before, and who had danced with her as though he could not stop himself.

Percy, whom she had long ago resolved never to want. All those years telling herself that she could never forgive him, and here she was, allowing the press of a hand, the touch of his mouth, to vanquish all of that.

She wished she had done it sooner.

She didn't know she'd been crying until she put her hand to her cheeks and felt the tears.

Percy produced a handkerchief from somewhere. "Was it so very bad, sweet witch?" he murmured, his words a drug.

Cecily reached for the anger that had sustained her through four years of matrimony, only to find it was a storm that had blown itself out.

"No." She hated the way her voice cracked a little. No, it had not been so very bad.

He reached for her hand, taking it in his. Although they had held hands all evening, this felt different somehow, when their bodies were otherwise so far apart. His skin was warm against hers, the callouses on his palm rough against hers. She recalled the way his fingers had scraped against the page of his book as he concentrated, and her stomach fluttered helplessly. *How* such an act could be so seductive, she didn't know, but she couldn't deny the heat that corkscrewed through her body, ending between her legs at the thought of those hands on her.

Stomach, breasts, lower. Lower.

It had been an age since he had last touched her there. Even then, the encounter had been short-lived, because she had not wanted him to be in her bed, so before anything of that nature could happen, he had left.

How ridiculous that she'd been denying herself because of a man who'd never wanted anything more than her innocence.

The blow was crippling.

"Circe?" he asked, and it sounded so like her name when he said it like that. "What's the matter?"

I'm a fool. But not just a fool—one who had hurt her husband so much she couldn't be certain that this one night of dancing would be enough to bring him back.

His thumb swept across her inner wrist, urging her into speech with that kind, patient way he had. Even when she knew she was being a brat.

The carriage pulled up to the house, and her heart clenched. This was the end of Odysseus and Circe; now they must return to being Percy and Cecily, with all the complications that went along with that.

He released her hand, and she felt the loss like she had lost the hand itself.

"We have arrived," he said.

"When we step inside?" She couldn't hide the plea in her voice—though for what, she couldn't be entirely sure. "What then?"

"Then?" He inhaled slowly, and softness crept back into his voice. "Ah, my sweet love. Then we will have to face the dawning of the day." He rose, crouching a little in the confined space, and leant in close. Certain she would receive another kiss, Cecily closed her eyes. But instead of her lips, his mouth ghosted across her cheek. "Goodnight, my darling," he whispered.

Tears, as unexpected as they were inconvenient, stung her eyes, and she remained where she was, hands entwined tightly in her lap, as Percy climbed out of the carriage.

By the time she, too, entered the house, his figure had long gone.

Chapter Eight

Chapter Eight

Cecily woke with an aching head. For a long time, she lay in her bed, staring at the ceiling. Last night had been . . . it had been . . . Well, it had been eye-opening. When Percy was not Percy, she liked him. Perhaps she always had.

Before last night, she'd assumed he would continue his mission of avoiding her at every given opportunity, and ending their marriage in all but name. But last night he had come for her. Followed her. Danced with her, flirted with her, *kissed* her. Ardently.

And she . . . Well, she had no desire to return to the way things had been.

Which meant, logically, that she would have to go about changing them. Perhaps Percy would also come to that conclusion: he wanted her, and she wanted him, and she did not wish to be married to anyone else. That, surely, would be enough to welcome her back into his life. They could talk about music again. Or myths and legends that they'd both familiarised themselves with. Or, perhaps, sing.

Impatient, because it was almost noon—though they had arrived home past dawn—she rang the bell for her maid. If she was lucky, Percy wouldn't have risen yet, and they could breakfast together for the first time in over a week.

Had it really only been that long? It felt like a lifetime.

She stumbled out of bed and rubbed her eyes, trying to think of what she would tell him. That she wanted more from their marriage than she had ever done before. And, she supposed, to hope that he felt the same way.

Though she dressed quickly and hurried into the breakfast parlour, she entered the room to find it empty. She rubbed her eyes and stared at the neatly laid table, her place laid with precision and the folded newspaper beside Percy's place, a sure sign he had come and gone. Despite the fact she'd risen early to catch him.

Her newfound optimism deflated. Evidently he did not feel, despite the intimacy they're shared the previous night, that anything needed to change between them.

She turned to the footman by the door. "Where is Sir Percy?"

"I believe he went out for the morning, ma'am."

"I see." No longer hungry, Cecily toyed with the laced edge of her sleeve. "Do you know when he will be back?"

"I'm afraid not, ma'am."

The old Cecily would have flounced out, determined to spend not one single thought on her errant, and notably absent, husband. But that had been the Cecily who hadn't experienced the subtle thrill of her husband's hands on her.

They really had to talk about that.

She glowered at his empty place setting. Difficult to talk to a man who had fled at the first opportunity.

Very well. If that was how he intended to be, she would not offer him the opportunity. They *would* discuss this, and without the distractions of London and all it had to offer. Let him avoid her while trapped in a carriage. Perhaps *then* they might have a conversation.

A tiny voice whispered in the back of her head that it was too late—she had already lost him—but she quashed it determinedly. Percy still wanted her. Perhaps he did not love her now, but he wanted her. And she wanted him. Perhaps *she* did not love him—she did not know how to, or what love even *was*—but that didn't matter.

She would not allow this to be the end. Percy had done enough saving of their marriage. Now it was her turn.

Wind tugged at Percy's hair as he urged his mount faster, across Battersea Common Ground and away from London, towards Clapham. Not Hyde Park today—he was not in the mood to promenade and exchange bows with all and sundry. No, this morning, unreasonably early, he needed a means to find his equilibrium.

That morning, as he'd listened to her prepare herself for bed, he'd stood by the door, willing himself not to go to her. Their relationship was fragile enough as it stood. Complicating it with physical advances he couldn't be certain she would accept was not the solution. He knew that.

At least, part of his body did. The other part, which had held most of his body's supply of blood, had been far more difficult to persuade.

Hence the brisk ride.

Once he returned, he would be in a better frame of mind to consider where the hell they were to go from there.

The streaming wind did much to cool the pounding of his blood, and by the time he reached Clapham and partook of a late luncheon and a tankard of ale, his mood had improved somewhat. Only to be dashed when he returned home and he found the servants bustling around, hauling his possessions about with abandon.

"Percy." Cecily herself stood at the top of the stairs, fiery curls tumbling a little haphazardly around her face. He longed to brush them back into place, but there was a fierceness to her expression he recognised all too well.

Boudicca, about to declare war.

He assumed an indifferent expression. If she intended to haul him over the coals for his behaviour the previous evening, he would be forced to remind her that *she* had been the one to kiss him. Admittedly, he had asked for it, but that was hardly the point.

"Cecily," he said, looking up at her.

A haughty brow rose. "You've finally returned."

He waved a hand at the scurrying servants. "What's the meaning of this?"

"It's summer."

"So I've observed, but that doesn't provide an explanation."

One hand in her skirts, she descended the stairs until she was only a few above him, their noses almost level. At this height, he could see the dark shadows around her eyes, and it took all his self-control not to touch her face in an attempt to ease the strain there. "I thought it was time to retire to Hollyhead."

He frowned. "Hollyhead? We hadn't intended to leave for another few weeks."

"Yes, well." Her mouth thinned. "I thought it might benefit us to leave earlier."

He searched her face, trying to find her reasoning behind her stubborn jaw. "Why the sudden change of heart?"

"Why not? Have you any desire to stay in London?"

Aside from a few loose ends to clear up and some invitations he would have to turn down, nothing. He could conduct all other business from Holyhead—as well she knew. "I thought you might, my social butterfly," he said.

Her jaw tightened. "I am perfectly capable of turning down a few engagements."

"So it seems."

She stepped closer still. "When we last spoke on the subject, you said you would spend the summer elsewhere."

Confused, he frowned. "Is that what you would prefer?"

"No. I wish you to return to our house with me." She raised her chin. "I will not accept no for an answer. We leave tomorrow morning."

Just a few nights ago, he would have fought her on this. Protected himself and his heart the only way he knew how. But she had given him hope as he'd rarely had reason to hope before. So, he inclined his head. "Very well."

"May I ask you something, Odysseus?"

He almost smiled. "Of course."

"Why did you come to the masquerade last night?"

"Because," he said, catching her gaze and holding it, "I thought you wanted me to."

She nodded once, abruptly, her hands clenched before her. He reached for them, smoothing out her fingers and rubbing the half-moon welts her nails had left behind. "How about a question in return? A truth for a truth?" At her nod, he asked, "Why did you pretend not to know me?"

"Because you pretended not to know *me*." As though sensing he wanted more, she glanced away, throat working as she thought. "And because I thought it could be a chance to start afresh. To see what dancing would be like if you were not my husband but merely a man."

The very reason he'd allowed her to lead, allowed her to weave a new deception around them. One that abandoned the gauntlets they'd taken up in the days after their wedding. "And how was it?"

"It convinced me that I like the man."

"And not the husband?"

A line appeared between her brows. "I wish to reconcile the two." She glanced up at him, eyes pleading. "For you to be Odysseus, and for me to be Circe."

"I *am* Odysseus, love," he said, brushing his knuckles along her cheek. "I always have been."

"You *avoided* me this morning," she accused, a note of such petulance in her voice that he smiled.

"I had a lot to think about, and I needed space to do it with a clear head."

"You mean not with me?"

"You're distracting," he said, and was rewarded with one corner of her lips curving. "And last night, I . . ." *Wanted you so badly I could hardly breathe.* "I needed to know I was making the right decision."

"Which is?"

"I will not endure intimacy with a wife who is not wholly committed to me. But," he added before she could say whatever words were on her tongue, "if you work with me, I will work with you. Try, Cecily. Give me your word that you will try, and I will, too." He smiled, releasing her. "That's all I ask."

Her eyes were clear and bright, every shade of green. "Do you need me to love you? For you to stay?"

"I need you to at least want to," he said, his voice gravelly and low. She shivered. "I am not unreasonable, but I want you too much to be satisfied with a little. I will not settle for only part of you, or half measures. Either I will have all of you, or I will have none at all."

Chapter Nine

Percy arranged his legs so his knees didn't brush against Cecily's opposite him. Her travelling cloak lay discarded beside her as she peered out of the window. In prior years, she had left the travel arrangements to him, but this time, she had arranged almost everything.

To reward her efforts, he'd chosen to share the carriage with her rather than riding alongside, as was often his way. That was as far as he was prepared to go, however. If she wanted conversation, or to speak whatever was so obviously on her mind, she would have to do so of her own volition. So far, they'd been silent as they'd left London and changed horses.

Instead of making idle small talk, he laced his fingers on his chest and examined her in the hazy late-June sunlight. Soft auburn curls fell around her face, the ribbons of her bonnet pinning them against her cheek. She huffed one away, and he watched as the lock of hair fluttered in the wake of her breath.

Poetry had never been a form of expression that he had mastered—and now he lamented it, wished that he knew how to capture that tilt in her expression when she raised her gaze to his. That dawning realisation.

If he could, he would have wrapped it up in words and committed them to paper so he would never forget.

"I was thinking that we should extend the pond," she said.

He almost laughed. Instead of a heavy conversation about the future of their marriage, approached like a battleground scarred by past victims, she'd chosen to begin the conversation with this.

A pleasant surprise.

He arched his brows, giving her free rein, the way he would offer his horse its head. "The pond?"

"Yes. I read a book recently about duck husbandry."

He could barely contain his smile. "Naturally."

"It befits my position to have an opinion about household matters."

"Of course. And what matter is more a lady's domain than ducks?"

"Are you laughing at me?"

"Never." The curl of a smile escaped his lips, and he wrestled his expression back under control. She would never know how lovely she looked when she scowled, all dark beauty like storm-clouds and rain on a hot summer's day. She was lightning and thunder and everything that was fiercely lovely about nature, and he was the parched ground who so desperately needed to taste her.

A flush climbed up her throat and spread, blotchy, to her cheeks. "I thought you would want to be a part of a discussion on what changes I wish to make to your house."

"It's your house, too," he said gently. "Though of course I always value your opinion."

"Is that so?"

"I would be fascinated to hear more about these ducks."

Finally, a reluctant smile tugged at her lips. "Now I know you're laughing at me."

"Not at all. Tell me, in great detail, if you please, your intentions for the pond. Do you have any other plans? I thought perhaps we could extend the orchard. I have a hankering for plums."

Her nose wrinkled. He rather wished he could kiss it. "Plums?"

"Do you dislike them?"

"My mother grew them." She spread her fingers across her skirts, smoothing the material. Percy was, confound him, reminded in rather vivid detail of what lay underneath. "We had plums with everything."

"Then we'll grow something else. Apples? I used to go apple-picking as a boy."

Her smile grew, though he saw her bite the inside of her cheek to prevent it from spreading any further. "And how many years ago was that?"

"Wretch," he said easily, not missing the way she glanced out of the window to hide her mirth. "What fruit would you prefer?"

"I like apples."

"Then apples it will be."

"How about an orangery?"

"This is a sudden and unprecedented interest in our garden." He tilted his head as colour spread fiery fingers up her throat. "Any particular reason why?"

"I thought I should—make an effort to be a better wife. I know wives are supposed to oversee these things."

"Forget whatever preconceived notions of what wives are supposed to do." His voice had hardened, and he made an effort to soften it. "I only want you to do what you're comfortable with."

"Yes. About that." Her colour only deepened, and she glanced away. No sign of Boudicca today; rather, she looked more fragile than he had ever seen her. "The masquerade."

He inhaled. "Yes."

"You kissed me."

The technicality—that she had been the one to initiate—did not seem worth mentioning. "I did."

Almost absently, her eyes fixed on a distant point, she brought her fingers to her lips, tracing them in a way that brought about a sudden and inconvenient bulge in his trousers. "I liked it."

"You did," he said, his voice lower, rough. "You liked it when I kissed you as Odysseus." He shifted in his seat, and her gaze dropped, catching at his groin and the erection he'd failed to hide. If her cheeks had been red before, now they burned, rioting against the vivid shade of her hair. "The question is," he continued, "why you won't allow yourself to kiss me like that when you're my wife?"

Cecily had known—of course she had—that the question was coming. It was a deserved one, and one that necessitated discussing a man she no longer wanted to think about.

"I am—" She looked at her hands, then back at him. He settled back into his chair, hands clasped around his stomach. By the looks of it, he intended to wait. For however long it took. An excellent choice, given she didn't know how to answer.

She spread her fingers across her skirts again, noting the way he glanced at them. His nostrils flared and he looked back at her, a light burning in the back of his eyes.

"I don't know how," she said quietly. "When we first married, I thought . . . I thought I only ever wanted to be with another man. Of course, I didn't have a choice in the matter, and I resented you."

He inclined his head. "I'm aware."

"I know you want a reason, or an excuse, but the truth is, I convinced myself I hated you for so long, it became easy to not . . . Respond. And at the beginning, I felt so angry with you, I told you I didn't want . . ." Her cheeks flamed. "Well, anything. Which you obliged. Then, later, even when you were pleasant, when you treated me well, I told myself I could never forgive you, and that you would never compare to William."

His jaw clenched. "I should have said more to turn you against him."

"No. I think . . ." She twisted her hands together. "The man I had in my head, the one I thought was William, doesn't exist. You didn't compare, because no man ever could. It was only when I discovered the truth . . . I'd been living a lie for so long." Her eyes stung and she closed them, willing the tears to remain in her throat and not break free of her eyelids.

"Then why Odysseus?" Percy murmured, his voice closer now.

"After William, it was a relief to dance with you. And as Odysseus, I didn't have to think of anything else." The tears gathered on her lashes, hot and wet, and she prayed they didn't fall. "No past. No future."

"Mm." His hand, warm against her cold skin, touched her face. "When I was someone else, you had forgiven me."

"I already had," she whispered. "I just didn't know it. I'm sorry for being so cruel."

His laugh ghosted along her cheek, and his arm slid around her shoulders, pulling her into his body. Dimly, she recognised that his thigh now pressed against hers, and he must have crossed the narrow space to her side of the carriage. But her face pressed against the curve of his neck as she leant into him, and the logistics of their position stopped mattering.

He smelt like home. Like woodsmoke and wool and cologne. His other hand came to cup her cheek, smearing away the wetness there. Her heart, which for so long had been dormant in her chest, gave a little lurch. Or perhaps a flutter. She wasn't well-versed in its movements, having never felt anything from it before. Yes, she had flirted—a great deal—but none of her beaus had meant anything to her. If anything, they were designed as punishment.

Look, I am still desirable, though you claimed me. I am not yours.

"Do you regret marrying me?" he asked. The same stupid, fateful question she had asked him. The truth sat on her tongue, though it took courage to utter it.

"No. No, I haven't for a long time now."

"Then at least I did something right." Something pressed against her head, his lips perhaps, even as he eased his arm away from her and returned to his position on the other side of the carriage. He raked a hand through greying hair, silvery strands falling back into place with careless dishevelment, and Cecily longed to run her fingers through it.

She thought over their interactions over the past few days. Their flirting as Odysseus and Circe, and his teasing of her now. His obvious attraction, so blatant it almost intimidated her. Every instinct told her that their marriage was salvageable.

He had not stopped wanting her when he retreated from her entirely.

For years, she had taken him for granted; she did not think she should continue to do so now.

I will have all of you, or I will have none at all.

The implication was clear: if she could not love him, or convince him that she did, then she may still run the risk of losing him, no matter how much he wanted her.

Fear struck through her.

He frowned, as though sensing the direction her thoughts had gone in. "What's the matter?"

"How am I to know?" she burst out. "How will I know if I love you?"

His smile was gentle, just enough that it made her want to cry all over again. "You will know, my witch. Love is not always what you think it ought to be, but when you find it—or it finds you—it will make itself known."

He spoke as though love were its own entity, something out of her control entirely. But she could not allow that to be the case—she would hunt this elusive love down, if that's what it took, so she could finally give Percy the life he deserved and the wife he wanted. She would *force* herself to love him, and then he would never leave her.

Chapter Ten

As they arrived at their inn for the night, Cecily was struck by the noise from the coach house. Ostlers bustled across the yard, and the sound of merriment and clinking emerged from the taproom, which appeared full. Percy handed Cecily down, his hand on the small of her back as he guided her inside. The innkeeper, once he discovered their identity, bowed obsequiously and led them to a private parlour on the second floor.

Cecily sank on to a chair by the fire, and Percy stood by the window, apparently deep in thought. She removed her gloves, chewing at a hangnail. Tonight, she would be sharing a bed with her husband. A chance for them to rediscover the intimacy they'd begun as Odysseus and Circe. Not only did her body long for it, but she was certain that if she had him in that way, she could convince him that she loved him—or at least, something close. It would be a hurdle overcome. Proof that this marriage would work.

Another reason for him not to leave her.

All she had to do was seduce him.

Percy turned, crossing the room until he stood before her, and removed her hand from her mouth. He smoothed his fingers over hers, lingering on the nail she'd bitten, and once again it reminded her of the book she'd watched him caress. The soft scraping of paper against skin. Heat rose in her core.

"Peace," he said, smiling down at her briefly. But before she could say anything else, or perhaps even start a conversation, he wandered away from her again, returning to the window and his contemplation.

To her relief, or perhaps her disappointment, dinner arrived promptly, and they took their places at opposite ends of the table. Percy seemed disinclined to conversation after their conversation in the carriage, so dinner, too, was silent. After a glass of wine they drank—once again in silence—before the rather unnecessary fire, Percy offered her his arm and they summoned a servant to take them upstairs.

With every step, Cecily's heart threatened to ricochet out of her chest. This was her moment. Perhaps it wasn't the most *auspicious* of locations for a seduction, but when they entered their room, it was spacious and the bed looked neat, turned down with white sheets. To be sure, she could still hear the roaring men from the taproom downstairs, and the snorting of horses from the stables, the chaos of arrival from another patron, stableboys calling to one another, voices coarse and friendly. And there was no guarantee that the mattress was comfortable, or that they seemed likely to find much sleep.

But this was the first time they were to share a bed in quite some time, and if she waited until they arrived at Hollyhead, they might return to separate rooms. She could envisage pressing her body against Percy's when they both occupied the same bed. Arriving in his room to enter his bed, and request the right to do so, seemed rather more of a challenge.

"I thought you might like a bath after the journey," Percy said, and she turned away from the bed to see the screen before the fire. And the steaming bathtub filled with hot water standing in front of the coals' glow.

A bath.

Her heart leapt into action, hammering against her ribs. This was it. She could ask him to remove her clothing—one had to be naked to enter a bath, which boded well for her plan—and surely things would progress from there.

"Was that presumptuous of me?" he asked when she said nothing. "I won't be here, Cecy."

"I—" She frowned at him. "What?"

"I wouldn't wish to make you uncomfortable. Take as long as you like. I'll give you plenty of time."

"What about you?" she asked desperately. "Would you not like to bathe?"

"Tomorrow evening we'll be home. I can last until then."

Not knowing what she wanted to say or do, Cecily took a step towards him. Candlelight played over the lines and edges of his face, half gilding him in gold and half in shadow. In a begrudging way, she'd always accepted he was handsome—but now, for some inexplicable reason, he took her breath away.

Had he always been so *tall?* So *broad?*

How unreasonable of him to spring these realisations on her now.

"You don't have to leave," she said. "If—if you do not want to."

"Oh?" He looked down at her, his expression unreasonable.

"If it would not be convenient, I mean. You must also be tired, from the journey, and I would not mean to keep you waiting for me outside somewhere when you could be—" Heavens, she was rambling. "I would not like to put you out," she finished lamely.

More to the point, it would be exceedingly difficult to seduce a man who was not there.

"How considerate of you." The very corner of a smile curled his lips before he tucked it away again, and she knew she had done something else to make him amused. It seemed to be happening all the time now, but she had lost the poise she had so painstakingly constructed over the course of their time together.

"Would you like me to stay with you, Cecily?"

"I asked for your benefit," she said helplessly.

"I do appreciate it. But now, you see, I am asking for mine. What would you like me to do?"

A sudden vision assaulted her of Percy's mouth on hers, his hands exploring her body with the same patience with which he did everything. The bed looked more inviting than ever.

Her fingers tightened in the material of her skirts as she blinked rapidly. Her throat was so desperately dry, but she had a sneaking suspicion that no amount of water would cure it.

"I—"

How *did* one seduce one's husband? It seemed a decided oversight that she had not, until now, thought to ask.

Kiss me, every muscle screamed.

"Would you undo my dress?" she asked, turning and presenting him with the laces.

"Certainly." Hot breath tickled her neck as he began unlacing, fingers quick and nimble. She'd never had anyone other than a maid undress her, and the sensation was entirely different. His knuckles lightly brushed her spine as he went, and she shivered as her dress fell open. A few hooks later and she could pull her arms through, letting it pool to the floor. Now she wore nothing but her chemise and stays, and when she turned to look up at him, the impassiveness on his face was gone, replaced by a burning she recognised. It struck something in her, too, a gong that sounded through her body, reverberating until *she*, too, burned.

Her face flamed; her fingers shook. He glanced down at her, the remaining layers of material hiding her body from him. Even so, her nipples pearled, visible through the chemise and stays. Temptation and nervousness. The desire for him to touch her, and the sudden urge to hide herself away.

Though she was not bare, she felt as though he saw every inch of her.

He stepped back, the space between them growing cold. "I'll leave you to your bath," he said. "A maid will see to you."

Left standing in the middle of the room, Cecily shivered, wrapping her arms around herself as the door closed and he was gone.

Percy was a coward. A lily-livered, good-for-nothing coward.

What he ought to have said was that he felt it would be better if they took things slowly, and certainly did not get carried away *here* of all places. He wanted to have her at Hollyhead, and the thought of it made him so impatient to leave, it was an effort for him to stay in place.

He wanted to take his time with her, to have all the privacy they could ever need. There were a multitude of things he wanted, and if this was to be their first attempt at intimacy since repairing their marriage, he did not want it to be *here.*

If he had stayed, he would have inevitably given in. Remaining and not touching her would have been impossible.

Thankfully, the taproom did not welcome or encourage such thoughts. The majority of its patrons were working men enjoying a meal away from home. Beer spilt onto the floor, which was padded with straw to catch such messes, and his elbows stuck to the table. The scent of tallow candles mingled with body odour and alcohol, the combination so potent he prayed it might have taken his sense of smell before he returned upstairs.

With a twitch of his fingers, he waved over another ale. He was going to need it.

By the time Percy ventured back upstairs, two hours had passed. There was no chance that Cecily could still be in the bath without looking like a prune, which meant he had averted the worst of it.

Or best.

He wasn't sure if he was doing himself a favour or tormenting himself beyond all endurance.

Probably both.

The room was dark, soft with the scent of roses that had no doubt been used in her bath. This was one of the better coaching inns along the Great North Road, and he was reminded of its quality as the floors barely creaked underfoot. Hopefully Cecily wouldn't notice his arrival, and especially wouldn't notice the rustle of fabric as he changed in the semi-darkness.

His valet would be horrified to know the manner by which he stripped, but that was a battle better had in the morning.

The sheets were cool as he slipped between them, and he congratulated himself on a job well done as he settled against the pillow.

Beside him, Cecily slumbered, just as he had hoped she would. No awkward questions, nothing but the scent of her for him to drown in, and the knowledge that barely two slips of material separated them.

As he so often did when he was around her, he hardened. Jasmine lingered in the air, clinging to even his damn pillow, and he wanted to hate it.

As he did with almost all things Cecily-related, he failed.

Heavens above, he was a ruined man. Ruined for her, ruined for all women but her. Incapable of sharing a bed with her without the most lurid fantasies replaying in his mind. Ones where she rolled over him, her body fitting against his the way he knew it was meant to. Nothing between them but breathless desire.

At the thought of her slickness sinking on to his erection, he near groaned. Nearly took himself in hand like an animal, although she was right there. Ordinarily, he had the time and space to sate his desires at least a little. Privacy in his room; more space between them than a matter of inches.

This was not an ordinary situation. And she had no idea what she did to him. For all her pretences that she was a woman of the world, she was still frighteningly innocent. Naïve about all the ways a man could want a woman. He'd shown her only a little, afraid of scaring her, and if she had been with another man outside of their marriage—

No, he wouldn't let himself believe it. Not with the way she stiffened whenever he touched her too intimately. Though, at her own confession, that stemmed from the way she disliked and resented him.

Had disliked and resented him. Perhaps now was different.

He throbbed, almost embarrassingly needy, and might even have left the bed in search of some relief when the sheets rustled. She rolled, tangled in the blankets, her hair loose and soft and slightly damp around her head, and pressed against him.

"Percy," she mumbled, still caught in sleep. Damn him, he wanted to wrap her in his arms. Bring her closer. Relearn her curves with all the ardency he had denied himself the last time.

She shifted, her movements clumsy, and brushed his hardness with her knee. He inhaled sharply, and the sound stirred her. She tensed for a second, and he could practically see awareness catching up with her mind. Then she relaxed again.

"It *is* you." One hand came to his face, fingers scraping the stubble that had grown there. "You came back late."

To avoid precisely this. So he wouldn't have to encounter any possibility of having her in his arms.

Once again, her leg brushed against his cock, and this time he couldn't help the sound—barely a sound. A growl, a moan. A huff of air. His hands found her waist, preparing to roll her back. But her eyes widened—curse him, even in the barely there light of the bedchamber, he could see that—and he felt the way she stiffened, body tensing against his. The only thing she wore was a nightgown, and the heat of her skin burned through it.

"Was that—"

"You should go to sleep, Cecily." His voice was tight, the restraint he had been carrying for so long fraying.

Her fingers twitched against his cheek as though she was also realising what position they were in. How close they were. Her breath shuddered free, dancing across his face.

The darkness was not helping. Perhaps if it was daylight, he could see all the ways this would be a bad idea. Instead, he was painting desire in her eyes, a wild, helpless want that matched his own.

"Percy," she repeated. Her nose brushed his, and she softened in his arms. The hand on his cheek travelled down until she cradled his jaw. "I've missed you," she whispered.

He was but a man. His mouth met hers in a wild, searing, half-desperate kiss.

Chapter Eleven

When he'd left the room before she'd so much as removed all her clothes, she had been certain she would not find a way to seduce him. Even now, half asleep as she was, she lost sight of her goal. His lips pressed hot against hers, tilting her head and opening her mouth so his tongue swept into her mouth.

For an instant, her mind woke up, tightening her muscles in instinctive response. But his hand travelled softly down her side, tracing her curves, and she forced herself to relax.

This felt good. Nothing, not all the conditioning she had put on herself, would take that away from them—her—now.

If she were to convince him of her affection, this would be necessary.

And, if she could find a way of enjoying herself, so much the better.

The kiss gentled, as though he was actively attempting to hold himself back, and Cecily gripped his shoulders, tugging him closer. Her thoughts tangled into knots, muddying with all the different things she wanted. Her knee nudged the hard ridge between his legs once more, and he let out another huff of air that travelled straight through her.

She would not deny her desire. Not this time.

Odysseus. Percy. The two men blended in her vision, blurring until she could not distinguish one from the other. The stranger, and the man she'd spent years resenting. The man in the mask, and the man whose face she knew better than her own.

Now she kissed his mouth, kissed his cheeks and the cheekbones there, kissed the graze of stubble along his hard jaw, kissed his forehead. Her chest felt oddly full, oddly tight, though she didn't know precisely why, only that this felt different from anything she'd ever experienced. Her body lit with every press of his hands, winding her tighter, tighter.

Occasionally, by herself, she had experienced a craving for something. Fullness. And she had never understood what it was she wanted.

Now she knew. She ached, empty and wanting.

Percy's hand slid to her backside, squeezing as he let out a muffled groan against her neck. Her mind emptied of all her plots and ploys. All that remained was her desperation to get his hands on her bare skin.

Lust was a frightening thing. She had been content. Now she was ravenous.

She nipped at his lip, urging another strangled sound from him, the knowledge that she was undoing all his careful restraint lighting her up inside. Brick by brick, his control came tumbling down, until the hand that gripped her hip slid her on top of him, right against the hard ridge of his arousal.

Her body moved before she gave it permission, and she pressed her aching core against him. Rolled her hips, rubbed, pushed until the friction made fireworks explode behind her eyes.

This was all right. This was good. This didn't involve any invasion of her body, it did not make her feel as though everything felt too much, too overwhelming. There were no inhibitions between them.

No, there was something else entirely.

Her nipples hardened almost painfully, her breasts heavy and aching.

Percy, his face a mask of strain and pleasure, eyes hazy and yet focused entirely at her, looked as though his jaw might crack. She rolled her hips again, drawing another groan from him—coming from so deep inside him, she felt it rumble through her. In a way, it sounded almost like pain.

His hands ran up and down her waist as though to calm her, sometimes gripping as though he intended to remove her from him again. The press of his fingers seared into her soul.

"Percy." Her voice was a whine, a sound she'd never heard coming from her lips. "I want—" She didn't know, not exactly, only that he had everything she needed. And for once, she felt as though he could give it to her. "Please."

He cursed, low and fluently, under his breath, and reached up her sides, thumbs skimming her ribs, until he reached the tender underside of her breasts. "Is this what you want?"

"Yes, I—I think so."

That same thumb slid over her peaked nipple, and she let out a squeak of surprise at the bloom of pleasure. The tension between her legs notched a little higher. All the other times they'd come together, he'd touched her, and although some part of her had enjoyed it, nothing had ever felt like this. In the end, just as he abandoned his place in her bed, he'd abandoned those attempts to please her. And so, as a result, this heat, the restless, needy coil in her lower belly, winding tighter with every movement of his hands and roll of her hips, was entirely new.

His nightshirt, damp from her arousal, served to prevent flesh touching flesh. And perhaps that was a good thing, even if the hollowness, the *wanting*, only grew with every brush of his hands against her.

Sweet torture. Delicious torment. Endless, unquenchable desire.

She wanted more, yet did not know how to ask for it.

"Please," she pleaded, only half aware of what she was saying.

He sat up, bringing his face closer to hers, but instead of her lips, he pressed his mouth against her breast. Hot, wet tongue dampened the material, sending another pang of pleasure through her.

"Percy." His name caught between her teeth.

"Take it," he urged, fingers flexing against her hip. "Take everything you want from me."

For years, she had been doing just that. How selfish. How short-sighted, when they could have been doing *this* for all that time.

Her breaths grew shorter. Fractured. He hissed through his teeth as she ground down on him; even though the layers of clothing, she felt him twitch. She felt half mad in her lust, like she had discarded every artifice she had been wearing. There was nothing between them but this mutual, desperate, all-consuming want.

He sucked her breasts, flicking her nipples with his tongue, cupping them with his hands, murmuring praise over and over, as though he was as lost as she. She already knew his restraint lay tattered behind them both. His hand at her waist urged on her, encouraging her to continue her gyrations against him even as her body trembled and her movements grew jerky.

Everything was out of control.

The pleasure in her body tightened.

"Please," he said, his turn to beg, though she didn't know what for. He thrust up into her, the movement seeming involuntary, as though he could not quite stop himself. "Please, Cecy. I want to see your face."

The heat gathered between her legs, pleasure that pulsed and tightened with every brush of his length against her folds. Closer, closer, until she could see nothing but the dim outline of his face, eyes locked on hers, every line of his features tense. He rocked against her again, or perhaps she rocked against him, and she broke.

An eruption of heat and pleasure, a river breaking its dam, rushed through her, roaring and almost violent in its intensity. She gasped, moaned, shuddered even as Percy told her to be silent, to be quiet, to say his name again because he needed her, he needed to hear her say it, and she thought perhaps she did, only she could be certain of nothing but the way her body felt, endless waves of perfect pleasure.

Only when it faded, when she came back to herself and found Percy's arms locked tight around her, did she realise that he was still talking. Murmuring about how perfect she was, how much he adored her, how much he wanted her, still wanted her, wanted everything. And she shifted against him again, the sudden flash of pleasure blinding.

Her breath trembled on its way out, and she moved again, testing her limits, wondering whether it was too much—if she could take it, if she needed space between them—when Percy moaned. The sound slipped from his lips like a prayer, or perhaps a curse, and he stiffened under her, his erection pulsating. Hot dampness soaked into the nightgown separating them, and after a belated second, she understood that he had reached his climax, too.

The last vestiges of sleep left her, and she buried her head in Percy's shoulder. His hand came to cradle her head, gentle despite his deep, panting breaths. Awareness slowly filtered through. She was straddling him, her legs on either side of his hips and his arms fully enfolded around her. The dampness between her legs wasn't unpleasant enough to encourage her to move—and she wasn't entirely sure she could, anyway. Her legs trembled and she felt as though the strength had drained from her limbs.

Well, that was . . . That was . . . It had been magical.

And it had been with her *husband.*

There was no difference between him and Odysseus, after all. No reason for her to lock up. Nothing to obstruct this delight.

"Are you all right?" he murmured, breath still a little shaky by her ear.

She had been the one to undo him.

And he had been the one to shred her into pieces and put them back together again.

She felt reborn.

"I think so," she said. "I—" She almost wanted to ask if this had been enough to persuade him to take her as his wife once again, in every meaning of the word. But perhaps, although she wanted it more than anything, it would be more tactful to wait.

Her entire body trembled. Tact had nothing to do with what she'd just done. That had been all lust.

His hand stroked along her hair again, and she realised belatedly that he was probably trying to quell her shaking. A laugh escaped her, though it quivered on the way out, and her nose stung.

Her intentions with seducing him had been to convince him to want her—all parts of her. She'd been certain that if he knew she would give him everything as a wife, then he would be content to take her back. Take up the reins of their life as though he had never let them drop. What she hadn't anticipated from the act was this sense of vulnerability. As though he had cracked her chest open to reveal her still-beating heart. A violent sensation, though he had been nothing but gentle. And now she felt as though she were bleeding all over him.

She'd wondered what the sensation of love felt like, and now she wondered if it was this—this *fear* of losing him, this overwhelming sense of being open when she had spent so long trying to close herself.

If this was love, she didn't know if she wanted it.

She wasn't sure if she could live without it.

"Talk to me," he murmured. "Tell me what's on your mind."

She buried her face in his shoulder. "I don't want you to leave."

"To leave?" The hand stroking her hair stilled, holding her against him. "What do you mean?"

"I don't want you to decide I'm not worthy as a wife."

"Cecy—"

"I know I've not always been . . .what you wanted—but if you give me a chance, I will make it up to you."

"Cecily," he said, attempting to ease back, but if he saw her face, all would be lost. "The problem was never that you aren't what I want."

"The problem has always been that I am not what you thought I could be."

By his stillness, she knew she had found her mark. "All I ever wanted from you was your love, my darling."

And in all their years, she had done nothing but deny him.

"Can you forgive me?"

"It's already done." He nuzzled the side of her face, warm lips brushing her ear. She squeezed her eyes tighter, knowing tears beckoned, but not wanting to cry after such an act, in case he thought she'd returned to her own ways, determined not to enjoy the things he offered her. "Can you forgive me?"

"Whatever for?"

"I meant to take my time with you. Take you in *my* bed." He gave a wry, not entirely steady laugh. "This was not precisely that."

"I *wanted* you to lose control," she admitted, and this time, when she looked at him, she wasn't afraid. "And I think—I think I don't have to pretend that you are Odysseus."

His breath released as though she'd punched his gut. "No?"

"You are my husband, and you love me."

In the light, it appeared as though his eyes glistened. "Very much."

"How do you know?"

Those tear-softened eyes searched hers for a moment, and then he urged her off his body. "Let me clean myself up and we can talk."

Talk. A single word had never sounded so menacing before.

Still, she shuffled up against the pillow, watching as he lit a candle, the glow glinting off his silvering hair. Twenty years separated them, and she had once thought it an impediment, but now she admired the wisdom it gave him. The patience. She'd never appreciated what a gift his love was, no matter how foolishly bestowed. A man of her own age, a man ten years his junior, might have given up on her already.

But here he was, standing in this sparsely decorated room, cleaning himself with a washcloth. With a sigh, he abandoned his nightshirt entirely, tossing it to the side of the room and returning to her naked. This was—surely it couldn't be the first time she'd seen him without his clothes, but she'd never appreciated it before. The strong lines of his shoulders, the way his curling, dark chest hair greyed the same as his hair. The softness around his waist that she'd felt under his nightshirt but had never truly seen until now; when they'd married, she suspected that he'd been made up a little differently. Four years had taken their toll on his body, but as he approached her, she reached out her hands.

He watched her gravely as she rested her palm against his heart, its beat a little elevated, and rested the other on the rounded curve of his stomach. Underneath, his length lay limp and spent under a still-dark thatch of hair. Though, as she watched, it appeared to thicken slightly.

His laugh was rough as he took her chin and tilted it to him. "No more time for that tonight, love."

Love. The word cut through her, hitting those same chords as before, the echoes speaking its own melody. And she knew. She *knew.*

"I think I do," she blurted, her hands still on his body, her eyes on his. "I think I do love you, Percy. I just didn't know until this moment."

Chapter Twelve

Percy stared at his wife. Four years of heartbreak, and now he was hearing the words he'd spent so many hours dreaming on her lips.

I love you.

He couldn't quite bring himself to believe it.

He sat heavily, and although Cecily appeared almost ghostly pale in the single flame of the candle, he thought he saw her smile. Dazed, he slid the hand on her chin to cup her face. "Do you mean it?"

"I thought love was—" She frowned as she looked away, eyes distant. A little lost, even. "I thought it was how I felt when I met William. But it's not like that with you. Well, that is, sometimes it does feel like I'm floating—it did when we . . ." Her throat tightened with a swallow, and he stared at it, knowing it was almost unseemly for a man of his age to have so lost himself to desire, but here it was. His wife undid him in every conceivable way. "But then I felt other things."

Her eyes, shockingly dark in this light, returned to his. "So many other things. I thought love would be simple, but there is nothing simple about this. I'm only just discovering these parts of myself. And I'm afraid."

He knew the fear that came with love; he'd been feeling it every day for years.

He took the hand that rested on his stomach and brought her knuckles to his lips. "Love is not always easy, and it is not always the beautiful, pleasant thing you read about in novels. Sometimes, it is the very darkest parts of ourselves, the worst pieces, brought to the light. With you, I am hungry, and I am jealous, and I am always scared—not of losing you, but of never having you the way I always dreamt."

Her gaze slid downward, to where he twitched, already half hard again. Perhaps he was an old man compared to her, but his body made him feel young again—or perhaps she did.

Even so, he wanted her elsewhere, not here.

"Not yet," he said, kissing her knuckles again, then leaning in to kiss her soft lips. She responded with more enthusiasm than he'd been expecting, and he hardened fully. "Let's wait until we're home and in my own bed."

She raised her brows. "Isn't it customary for a gentleman to visit his *wife's* bed?"

"Perhaps." He drew her down beside him, tucking the covers around them both. They were on their way home, and his wife loved him. The tension he'd been carrying since he'd lost control eased into relief. "But I would rather have you in my bed. And then, you see, I would rather have you remain the rest of the night with me."

After a moment, she relaxed into his embrace. "Is that customary?"

"Frankly, my dear, I don't give a damn."

This time, when he kissed her, she gave up on any attempt at conversation.

In the morning, certainly for the first time in a long time, Cecily awoke with her husband beside her, his body pressed against hers. At first, she felt nothing but contentment. Then, as she remembered the previous night—the things she had done and the way she'd behaved—panic flooded her. She tensed, remembering the wanton way she'd gasped and moaned and rubbed herself against him. The way she'd come apart in his arms.

If her mother only knew how little she had behaved like a lady . . .

His arms tightened around her. "Don't even think about running," he said, his voice still rough from sleep.

Heavens above, she had told him she loved him. And she'd meant it. All this worrying about what love meant, what it felt like, and when the realisation had come, it had been a quiet knowing. An understanding of the world that, until then, had been denied to her.

Love, at least with Percy, was not the wild, unrestrained thing she'd imagined it to be with William. It was not found in overblown compliments and insincere flirting—it was here, pressed against her husband's chest, his breath in her hair, and a sense of contentment that soaked through her like her warm bath.

"Cecily?" Percy's hand moved up her arm. Then down. "How do you feel this morning?"

"Mm. Good." She touched the arm that banded around her stomach. "You?"

"Mm." She heard the smile in his voice. "Good."

"I do have a question."

"Oh?"

"Can we do that again? When we return home?"

He eased her around, turning her until she lay with her head on the pillow inches from his. In this light, his eyes appeared more green than brown. Just like hers. His hair, tangled and messy, fell across his forehead, silvery strands catching the light, and stubble grazed his chin. He was as imperfect as her in the morning. A new revelation, and one she delighted in.

His body did not resemble that of the Greek statues she'd seen, but she found she preferred the lack of chiselled perfection. He was human. Delightfully so, his skin occasionally rough but always warm, with arms that made her feel safe and eyes that saw straight through her.

"That depends," he said with the ghost of a smile, hand still resting on the curve of her hip, right where she knew her hipbone jutted out. "Have you changed your mind about loving me?"

"Can one change one's mind about that so soon?"

"Not if they meant it to begin with."

"I did," she said, with more confidence than she'd initially felt, but the more she reflected on it, the more right it seemed. "This is new for me. I've never been in love before."

"Not even with William Devereaux?"

"No," she said firmly. "I thought I was, but I was mistaken."

"I'm very glad to hear it."

"What about you?"

"This is my first time being love, too."

"Truly?"

He smiled. "Truly."

"Oh." She pressed a hand to his heart once more. "So you won't leave?"

"Would you like me to?"

"No," she said, too fast.

"Well then." He bent to kiss her, and she marvelled at the feeling of his mouth against hers—the certainty that this would become more familiar to her than breathing.

"Well then," she said, and kissed him back.

Considering this was not the first time Percy had lain with a woman, he rather suspected his eagerness was unseemly.

Then again, was there anything more indicative of youthfulness—a rarity at his age—than unseemly eagerness to remove one's wife's clothes? He thought not, and so he took no pains to hide his impatience, only submitting to dine when they arrived at Holyhead because the cook had been good enough to provide a large meal.

Cecily, for her part, picked at her dinner like a baby bird, declining most courses. He ate heartily, as he often did—though he found that with age there was a far more direct correlation to the amount he ate and the size of his waist—but his mind was elsewhere. Partially upstairs, and partially consumed with the distance between him and his wife.

At the beginning of their marriage, dining at opposite ends of the table had felt like a necessary formality. He could not entirely rule out the possibility that she might choose to hurl a knife at him and begin her life as a fugitive.

Now, he flattered himself, such an event was unlikely.

She cocked her head at him. "You're staring at me."

He raised a brow. "Should I not stare at my wife?" His gaze dropped to her plate. "You haven't eaten very much."

"I'm not hungry."

"No?" He met her gaze. "A shame. I am very hungry indeed."

Her eyes smouldered. To think this was the same girl who had never once reached her climax with him, no matter how patiently he applied himself to her. Truly, things had changed. Though, he reminded himself, he should keep in mind that he should go slowly with her, no matter her newfound enthusiasm.

He pushed back his plate. "Shall we retire?"

"Do you not intend to meet with your steward?"

Usually, that was one of the first things he did on reaching his estate. And, no doubt, his steward was even now expecting a summons. Quite possibly had put his work to one side in anticipation of a meeting.

Yet, all these things seemed less pressing than seeing to his wife.

"I can do that later," he said. "Tomorrow."

Her cheeks turned rosy. "Tomorrow?"

He nodded at the footmen that lined the walls. "Thank you. That will be all."

They bowed and left the room, and finally they were alone. Perhaps under other circumstances, he might have been tempted to have her against the table, but they had not progressed so far yet; he did not want to push things.

"Let me be clear," Percy said as he rose, approaching her. She pushed back her chair and stood to meet him, though he stood tall enough to look down into her face. He secretly loved the size difference between them, and the way she could control him with just one look. "I intend to take you upstairs, and I do not intend to relinquish my claim on you until the morrow. Will that be a problem?"

Her eyes glittered with too many emotions for him to read. Freckles scattered across her nose, and her fiery curls bobbed as she nodded her head slowly. "I have no objection."

"I'll be gentle," he promised as he left the room, her hand tucked firmly in his arm.

"You do not need to be."

"Yes, I do." He glanced down at her. "This is new to you. Is it not?"

She glanced down. "It is."

Relief spiralled through him that she had not been intimate with anyone else. That this time—now—would be her first time.

She turned her attention to the paintings on the walls. Her expression turned contemplative.

"Do you know, I think I finally feel at home here." She smiled a little as she nudged him with her shoulder. "Before, I would come here in the summer and count the days until we could return to London."

"And to all your engagements, my social butterfly?"

"You must confess the country is sadly devoid of company."

"A sad thing for a husband to hear."

She laughed, the sound airy and light—so different from any of the laughs he'd heard her give over the past four years. "None of my married friends, you know, rely on their husbands for company."

"Perhaps they married the wrong gentlemen."

"Perhaps," she conceded. "I suspect neither party has any desire to spend time with the other. Save Arabella, of course. She dotes on her husband. I always thought it odd."

"And now?"

"I suppose I can see the appeal." Her voice was so warm that he looked down at her. Beautiful, vibrant, alive, she watched him with amused affection. "And I am fortunate you dote on me, too. Another man might have given up on me for good."

"I was about to."

"I know. I think that was what spurred me into realising I wanted you. That, and knowing how it could be between us when I was not so caught up in the past."

They finally reached his bedchamber, and he pushed the door open, guiding her inside and closing it behind them. Want pounded through his body, too potent for words.

"Let me kiss you," he said gruffly.

She tilted her head so he looked down into her face. Then she reached up, removing the pins in her hair until her curls tumbled down her back, loose and a little tangled. Her eyes looked like the sunlit ocean in the fading light from the windows, holding untold depths. If he tried, he could swim forever and never reach the bottom.

"Percy." She smiled, soft and slow, and the last of the barriers around his heart, the ones he had erected to keep himself safe, cracked into dust. He was irrevocably, irrefutably hers, and there was no pretending that he could save himself now.

"You have my heart," he told her, sliding his hand along her jaw, his thumb coming to cup her cheek. "Forever, Cecily. Until the tides turn back on themselves and the moon outshines the sun. Until the earth crumbles into the sea. There is no world in which I don't love you, and no lifetime in which I ever stop trying to be a man who deserves you."

She placed her finger against his lips. "Until my last breath."

"Until my last breath," he vowed, and kissed her.

Chapter Thirteen

Cecily found that now it had come to it, being intimate with her husband for the first time in a long time, she did not want to wait. As he kissed her, she moved against him. Her experience had taught her certain things—no matter how unwilling to learn she had been, she could not have missed his preoccupation with her breasts. The way his gaze had lingered, feasted. The way his hands always came up to cup them, fingers swiping over her nipples in an attempt to induce her to respond.

A wave of shame flooded her, but not because of what they were doing. Rather, because of how she'd been with him.

The instant he felt her tense, he pulled back and away. His eyes glittered, his breath already coming fast, but he held her gently, as though she were made of glass. "We don't have to," he said, a frown touching his eyes as he searched her expression. "Or we can go slowly. I—"

"I don't wish to go slowly." She took his hand and placed it on her breast, feeling the way his fingers flexed, the slight hitch in his breath. Heat pooled in his eyes, matching the heat that throbbed between her legs.

Want.

Everything about this felt new, even though they were dancing to an old, familiar tune. All because she no longer resisted the response of her body to him.

"I'm sorry I made you feel as though I didn't want you," she whispered.

"Sweetheart—"

"Today will be different."

He trailed his finger down her neck, pausing at the neckline of her gown. "Today, I would like to teach you what—what it can be like."

Teach her. She liked the sound of that. "I'll prove a willing student."

"If you would ever like to stop, you must tell me."

"I will, but Percy, I won't want to stop."

"An easy promise to make before we've begun."

She smiled, pressing up against him so his hardness pushed against her stomach. "I want you," she said, watching at the way his eyes darkened at the words. His tongue moistened his bottom lip, and she shuddered at the thought of its liquid heat against her skin. "And I think—I *know* I love you."

The corner of a smile tilted his mouth as he kissed her jaw. "Are you certain, Circe?" he murmured, and something warm erupted in her chest. "Are you *certain* you love me, sweet witch? Or are you saying whatever is necessary to lure me into bed?"

She wrapped her arms around his neck. "Is it working?"

"I think you should say it again."

Happiness. She hadn't known it would be so potent, or make her feel so *giddy* with it. "I love you, Percy Somerville."

He nipped her collarbone in reward. "Good."

"I love you, husband." His erection throbbed against her, and she smiled. Evidently he liked the way she said that a *lot.* "Husband," she repeated, and he twitched again.

"I love you, wife." He picked her up and carried her to the bed, plopping her down on the mattress with surprising ease. Then again, she had always been particularly small against him. She loved that feeling of smallness now. Her softness against his solidness. His weight on her. Between her legs.

Then he flipped her, so she lay on her stomach. "Wife," he murmured. "Wife."

"Husband." Cecily gasped as his fingertips brushed her spine. Slowly, slowly, he undid the back of her dress. Then the laces of her stays. She expected him to turn her back around, but instead he kissed the back of her neck, moving her hair aside until he reached skin. At the same time, a hand explored her legs, sliding underneath her skirts.

Infuriating pressure. Infuriating man to take so long to give her what she'd finally admitted her body wanted.

"You are so beautiful," he said against her skin, and briefly allowed her to feel what she was doing to him, his hips grazing her backside.

"Then why are you taking so long?" she complained.

"Impatient, love?"

"Yes."

He laughed softly, and cupped her bottom before easing her dress up her legs. She wore too many layers, but he removed them with ease, and she helped, drawing herself up so he could tug them free. Her hair fell messily around her face when he had done, and she glanced over her shoulder at him, grinning through the tangled red that obscured her vision.

"An enchantress indeed," he said, a little hoarse as he brushed her hair aside. "You know, it was your hair I noticed first."

"Truly?"

"Truly." He turned her, sitting her shoulders against the pillow and leaning over her to kiss her mouth softly. Then, as she arched her back against him, longing for the feel of *something* against her aching breasts and sensitive nipples, he deepened the kiss, his tongue sliding into her mouth, where she met it with hers. He groaned.

"I want your clothes off," she said as she broke away, almost astounding herself with her boldness.

His smile turned into a smirk. "Be my guest."

Intriguing. She had never been the one to remove his clothes before—most times, he'd been wearing very little, and had removed it before joining her. How bizarre that four years of marriage had given her no better understanding of men's clothing. She fumbled with the buttons of his coat and waistcoat, tossing them aside. He helped her remove his shirt, tugging it over his head. Then came his breeches, her work already impeded by the large bulge that distorted the material. More than that, as she unbuttoned his falls, he made a noise that could only be described as a hiss every time her fingers passed over it.

She experimented by doing it again, and he sucked in a breath, the sound coming from his chest almost a rumble. Then, through the material of his breeches, she took hold of his length. Squeezed.

He caught her wrist. "Peace, my love," he said with a wry smile. "Let's finish your education in men's clothing before all your hard work goes to waste."

She frowned, trying to piece together the meaning of his words, but he merely gestured to the half-finished buttons. She completed them—there were only three—and he helped her remove them.

Then he sat before her, naked as she, and took her hand, toying with her fingers. "I know I am not as young as I was, or as spry," he said, tenderly, "but I will show you pleasure if you allow me that right."

Cecily leant in, pressing her mouth against Percy's, her other hand running down his chest until she encountered the wet tip of his erection. "I always found you handsome," she said, her breasts brushing his chest. This time, she was the one to suck in a breath. "Even if I could not admit it to myself at the time."

He urged her closer with a hand to the small of her back, and she obeyed, finding a way of sitting with her legs around his waist, their bodies pressed together with no room between them, her sensitive centre rubbing against his length. Every contact sent a burst of pleasure through her like sparks.

He kissed her, and she relaxed against him, no longer thinking about her figure, and whether he would find its sharp angles appealing. All she thought about was their bodies, and what they could do to one another. What they already did. What she *wanted.*

He broke away, panting, and she had the impression that even though they were barely moving, barely rocking against one another, he was already close.

And she—yes, she felt the way her body tightened in anticipation of her climax's arrival. As though he held the reins of her pleasure, and with each flick, he commanded it closer.

"Is this good for you?" she asked, moving against him and matching his rhythm. This position was both heaven and torture; they were so close that she could not move very far, but each tiny motion turned to fire in her veins.

Her hips tilted, and he almost slid inside.

The need to be filled swallowed her whole, and she whimpered in frustration.

He brushed a curl back from her eyes, and she realised he was trembling, too.

"We should discuss children," he said.

The incongruity of the statement took her entirely by surprise. One did not, she presumed, engage in these kinds of activities and think about children. Or, indeed, or anything other than one's partner.

He laughed at the expression on her face, and the movement almost slipped him inside her again. With what appeared to be great effort, he shifted, and the rub of his hardness through her slickness made her shudder, thoughts scattering.

"If you do not wish for children yet, then that changes—ah—things." His words sounded strained now. "How we should go about this."

"You've never asked before."

"Forgive me." He kissed one freckled shoulder. "I ought to have done."

Children. Instinctively, she thought about her mother, and her movements stilled, ardour dampened. She hadn't considered children, except to assume they would inevitably have some, and then to assume that they would not, given his lack of dedication in that area. This was . . . unexpected.

And yet, when she considered it, her heart thrummed at the thought of bearing Percy's children. Perhaps she would have a red-haired girl with the soul of a dreamer and her father's patient eyes—and heavens above, she *wanted* that. Wanted it more than she could ever have articulated.

"Yes," she said, and canted her hips. He slid in, just a few inches, and both their bodies tightened at the intrusion. The pleasure. The overwhelming sensation of being stretched. "Please."

"I should have readied you," he said hoarsely. "I intended to go slowly and show you everything, but—" He slid in another inch, and she ground against him, needing more, needing so much more, needing everything he had to give.

"I'm ready, I'm ready for you."

He gave a shaky laugh, forehead against hers. "You barely so much as know what that means."

She had vague, undefined memories of Percy readying her before, using his fingers on her—and on one occasion, his mouth, until she had wiggled away from him and begged him never to do that again. She also recalled the way her body had reacted. Its wetness. The dull edge of desire that she'd tucked away, trying to force herself to forget.

Now, that edge was honed and sharp.

"I'm ready," she insisted, and shifted closer, that final movement seating him fully in her.

They both took a moment to breathe, sharing each other's air. Then she kissed him—or perhaps he kissed her—with enough clumsiness that their teeth clacked together. They both laughed a little, but breathlessly, their bodies undulating as they found a rocking rhythm. Him inside her, filling her and stretching her, the pressure just enough that she thought she would explode, the sensation gathering in her lower belly. His kiss mimicked the roll of his hips, the give and take, the slick pleasure of it. They were joined so deeply, she lost track of where she ended and he began, and perhaps that was the beauty of it—beauty she'd never considered before, because her marriage to Percy had never felt like a *union* until recently. And this, she understood now, was the greatest union of all.

Once, she might have been ashamed of the noises she made, the way she sank her teeth into his shoulder, and the way that only inspired him to take her faster. Harder. More and more until her vision blurred and the tension in her limbs tightened beyond all reason, until she hovered on a precipice, coiled so tightly she knew she might snap.

"Cecily," Percy groaned into her skin. Dimly, she registered that it was damp, and that they were both covered in a fine mist of sweat, but it seemed an unimportant detail at the present. "Are you close, my darling?"

Yes. She hovered on a knife's edge. Every small, vital movement bringing her closer, but she didn't want to fall.

"Cecily." His voice was more urgent now, fingers digging into her thighs as he brought her to move still faster against him. "I need you to come for me."

Her inner muscles trembled, and again as though he held the reins, at his command she tumbled off her cliff into somewhere weightless and empty, filled only with pleasure so bright and shocking, she hardly felt the way she shuddered around him, or the way he said her name and thrust into her one final time as he found his own release, spilling inside her.

When she back into herself, she found him stroking her hair and smiling faintly. Her thighs shook, and he held her tightly.

"That was . . ." She didn't have the words to describe how that had been. *Incredible, awe-inspiring, wonderful* didn't quite seem to do it justice. "Thank you."

"No need to thank me, love." He kissed her hair. "I enjoyed myself as well."

"And now I may be in danger of conceiving a child?"

"Danger isn't perhaps the word I would use, but there is a chance, certainly. Have you changed your mind?"

She shook her head. "No. I think it would be charming to have a child with you."

He laughed, open-mouthed and delighted. And she laughed with him, enjoying the shudder of his chest, the way his mirth reverberated through her body.

"I think I must be dreaming," he said, and kissed her again. "Can this be real?"

"I don't think my imagination is so vivid."

"Nor mine, though it comes close." His fingers trailed up and down her spine. "I've dreamt about this so many times."

"Then perhaps we can make those dreams come true?" She raised her brows.

"Perhaps, though you must afford this old man a little time to recover."

"You have not behaved like an old man much of late."

"You make me feel young again," he said, and the smile that spread across his face was the most beautiful sight she'd ever seen. She traced the lines that flared from the corners of his eyes. To think she'd ever assumed she could not want him, crave him, love him.

"I love you," she said quietly, and his gaze turned serious, though no less lovely. A warmth so bright that it bathed all the parts of her life she would rather forget. Even if she had the choice, she would not have exchanged it for a thousand years, for a younger husband, for anything other than this, right here, with him.

He touched the ring on her finger, the one she had always worn even when she thought she didn't want to be married. Then he returned his gaze to her face. "I, Percy Somerville, take thee, Cecily Somerville—"

"What are you doing?" she protested. "We're already married."

"—To be my wedded wife, to have and to hold from this day forward," he said, speaking over her, his thumb still across the polished gold on her third finger, "for better for worse, for richer for poorer, in sickness and in health, to love and to cherish, till death us do part." His smile deepened. "You see. I have not forgotten."

"I hope you will do your fair share of having," she said, teasing even as her heart swelled. "And holding."

"Mm, and loving, I think."

"From this day forward," she murmured. "Until the end of time."

He laughed and kissed her again. "A little ambitious, my darling, but I'll do my best."

Epilogue

FOUR YEARS LATER

Percy crossed his legs as he watched Cecily take her place in front of the pianoforte, her stomach rounded with child, and three-year-old Lavinia Somerville climbing up onto the seat beside her.

"Here," Cecily said, showing their daughter where to put her fingers on the keys. "Now press gently. Gently, now. There you go, darling."

Lavinia, reddish gold curls tumbling down her back, grinned at her mother. Cecily smiled back, smoothing Lavinia's riotous hair from her face. "Sing with Papa," Lavinia commanded.

Percy stretched his legs out before him. "Do you not want to sing, Lavinia? You and Mama could sing together."

Lavinia pouted. "I like it when you sing."

Cecily raised her brows at Percy. "The general has commanded it."

"I had no clue our lives would be so dictated by such a small being," he grumbled, but he ruffled Lavinia's hair as he came to stand behind them, undoing Cecily's tidying. For all his complaining, he lived for these quiet moments, the ones after dinner and before Nurse came in to take Lavinia to bed. When it could be just the three of them—soon to be four—and they sang or read together. Already, Lavinia showed an inclination towards music, and once she began learning properly, she would be very talented. He suspected at least some of that came from all the times Cecily had cradled her and sang endless lullabies.

"What should we sing?" Cecily asked Lavinia.

"Something pretty."

Percy rifled through the pieces until he found *Robin Adair*, placing the piece before Cecily. She cast him a quick, appreciative glance that told him she had also not forgotten the first time they had ever sung together. Once, she had told him that it had marked the first time she began thinking of him in a different light, although those particular feelings had not come to fruition until several years afterwards.

For him, he could pinpoint the moment he understood the depths of his feelings to the first time he heard her sing. When her eyes had gone distant, and her voice had rung out, rich and sweet and flowing like a bubbling spring. She'd lost herself to the music, longing and passion a tangible thing inside her, and he had known then that she meant more to him than he had ever initially intended.

Of course, then he had not known that he would marry her; he'd assumed that his infatuation would pass. He should have known better.

Now, every time he heard her sing, it reminded him of how wrong he had been—and how much more he adored her now.

Lavinia put her chubby fingers against the keys and played a few notes, presumably in encouragement. Cecily laughed, and began to play. Just like that first time, he joined her, matching her voice with his. An elegant dance of sorts, his harmony wrapping around her melody, and she smiled the way she had that very first time.

Beside them both, Lavinia joined in, her sweet little voice following her mother's. Percy put his arms around them both. His family. How fortunate he was to have finally found the happiness he had always been searching for.

One day, when Lavinia was old enough to be married herself, perhaps she might sing to her future husband and attract his attention that way.

"There now," Nurse said from the doorway when they finished the song. "I believe it's time for your bed, Miss Lavinia. As for you, my lady. If I may say so, it's time for you to retire as well before you tire yourself out."

Cecily leant back against Percy, and he rested his hands against her shoulders. "I'll go up presently."

"Very good, my lady." Nurse turned her attention to Lavinia, who had already hopped down and seemed intent on fleeing to avoid her bedtime. "Now don't you try that with me, Miss Lavinia. You know my old bones can't take hunting for you under whatever chair you've hidden under this time."

"Lavinia," Percy said warningly. "Do as Nurse says, please."

His daughter huffed, jutting her bottom lip out in a parody of dismay. But she must have been more tired that she wanted to admit, because she didn't object to Nurse scooping her up, and instead rested her head against Nurse's shoulder.

"Can you tell me a bedtime story?" she asked as they left the room.

The door closed, but not before Percy could make out the answering, "Of course, Miss Lavinia."

Cecily sighed, her hands coming to cup her stomach. "I *am* a little tired."

"Then we'll retire." Bending, he picked her up, scooping her into his arms and carrying her out of the room.

"Stop! You'll drop me!"

"I may have a few years on you, but there's no chance of that happening."

She laughed, looping her arms around his neck. "Ever the romantic."

"If it's romantic to tuck my wife into bed and ensure she has something hot to drink, then I suppose I am."

"Don't be ridiculous, Percy. You must know that's *extremely* romantic." She sighed, nuzzling her face into his neck. "Whoever told me that bearing children would be the greatest gift on earth, I am convinced, never went through the trials of pregnancy."

"It won't be long now."

"Ah yes, until that far lesser trial of childbirth." She glanced up at him, eyes soft and warm with amusement. "I suppose it's a good thing that Lavinia is such a sweet, easygoing child, or I might think it's all for naught."

"If I could take that pain away from you, I would."

"I know. And I would freely give it." She giggled. "Alas, it's my burden to bear."

They reached his bedchamber, and he placed her carefully on the bed. There, he unlaced her shoes and she sighed with relief. Her ankles had swollen, and with her first confinement, she'd been self-conscious of all these changes. As though he could ever have loved her less for the ways her body changed—as though he ever allowed himself to forget what a miracle this was.

So bent and kissed her swollen ankles. "You are beautiful," he told her.

"I feel like a whale." She lay back, staring at the ceiling. "My mother wrote again today."

He paused his massage of her feet. "What did she say?"

"She requested to see Lavinia again, and to stay for the birth of this one." She traced her fingers across her stomach again. "I suppose she thinks that as you are a man, you're incapable of supporting me."

"Well, that's hardly an assumption you need to concern yourself with." He resumed his massage. "I distinctly recall you informing me last time that I could not, under any circumstances, leave you. I had to use the chamber pot on more than one occasion."

She pushed herself up on her elbows, looking past her bump at him. "You didn't tell me you had to use the chamber pot."

"My darling, you were in labour for half the night. I am still only human." He kissed the side of her calf. "And I would do it all again."

"Good. I have no intention of allowing my mother to replace you." She shuddered. "I told her no."

"Good."

"And I said that she could next see Lavinia when we are both in London, and only if Lavinia agrees."

If Percy had his way, he would have cut the woman out of their lives entirely. But for Cecily, even this marked a huge turning point in their relationship. After Lavinia had been born, she'd found it within herself to deny her mother the things which her mother thought were her right.

And he, keeping his personal thoughts to himself, encouraged her in whichever ways he could.

"I'm proud of you," he said.

Cecily's eyes fluttered closed. "I want our children to have a different life than the one I had growing up. She might be my mother, but she could be cruel."

Percy only stretched himself out beside her. "I know. But you've broken the cycle. Our children will be happy and loved. Now then, shall I get you out of this dress?"

"I think I may be a little too tired for that," she mumbled.

"I prefer to bed my wife when she is conscious and able to enjoy it, you ridiculous woman." He kissed the tip of her nose. "Come now. I'll call for a bath. Then you can have a glass of hot milk and go to bed."

"What about you?"

"I'll be right here, my darling. Until the very end of my days."

A small smile ghosted across her lips, even though her eyes never opened. "I love you, you know."

"I'm very glad to hear it." He stared into the soft, relaxed face of his wife, wondering how he could ever fully comprehend all the multitude of ways in which he was the luckiest man on earth—and how incredibly fortunate he was that this delicate, sweet wisp of a woman loved him in return. "I love you, too."

Thank you

Thank you so much for reading, dear reader. If you enjoyed this novella, I hope you'll leave a rating or review. It means so much to me as an author, and that support ensures I can keep going and writing books such as these.

It's important to me to write love in all its forms, and it was a privilege to write about Percy's enduring, steady, heartfelt love for Cecily. In a world of alphaholes, it was a breath of fresh air to write about a kind, compassionate man trying to make the woman he loves happy. To me, love is not an instant, not a look or a touch or the fleeting pass of feeling. Love is selfless and sacrifice and hard work—but it is also beauty, joy, delight, comfort. Sometimes, love is not what we think it ought to be—it can be quiet and reassuring and steady instead of the heady blaze of infatuation we often read about in novels. Often, that can turn into something deeper, too, and I enjoy both reading and writing it, but this novella came especially close to my heart. Just as Percy showed Cecily what love could be, so did my husband show me, and I cannot tell you what a privilege it was to write this into a story.

For more insights into my writing process, updates about my projects, and bonus scenes, sign up to my newsletter here: https://copperplate-newsletter.beehiiv.com/subscribe. Or, alternatively, visit my website at www.terrimackenzieauthor.com.

Don't forget to follow me on Facebook and Instagram. I share snippets of ongoing projects there!

Hope to see you around

Terri x

Acknowledgements

As always, I have the same old suspects to thank. This book could not have happened without the emotional support and beta-reading services of Rachel, Charlotte, Kelsey, and Amirah. Thank you for putting up with me being neurotic at every given opportunity, and for always telling me the multitudes of ways I could improve the novella. (Yes, Charlotte, the prologue was a good idea, and yes I KNOW you told me to put one in like three times before I caved.) Also, thank you all for falling in love with Percy as much as you did.

I must also thank a couple of readers of His Ample Desire! I fell in love with lovesick Percy from the first moment I (spontaneously) put him on the page, and I knew I wanted to give him his own story. But were it not for more than one reader coming forward and asking if he was to get his own book, I might not have tackled his book so soon—and I'm so glad I did! Writing his love story has been one of the greatest delights and privileges of my writing career thus far, and I adored writing a non-typical hero. Perhaps Percy isn't a duke, like Nathanial, or a boxer, like Jacob, an ex-soldier like Henry or a poet like George, but he makes up for all these 'shortcomings' through the constancy of his love. My ideal is not a man who can proudly display his rippling abs, or who battles a drinking problem through most of the novel (looking at you, Jacob). It's a man who knows how to love, and does so with his whole heart. So a huge thank you to everyone who pushed me into writing this novella next; it was a joy and a delight.

Writing romance has never been easy, and I have another thank you to offer two of my favourite writing groups. *Velvet Steel*, my favourite group of girls, thank you for writing with me, being unhinged with me, and feeding my ego even when most of you don't read histrom. I love you. *Historical Hoydens*, it has been a pleasure to hang out with a group of fabulous ladies all doing the same thing as me. Your encouragement, support, and camaraderie as we navigate the rocky road of publishing together has been invaluable.

I could not write acknowledgements without mentioning my husband. He will never read this—romances, especially of the Regency variety, aren't his cup of tea. But despite not being a reader (truly, his only flaw), he has been unfailingly supportive of me and my career from the very beginning. I could not have got where I am now without his encouragement and belief in me. And I could not have written Percy's love for Cecily without having experienced it firsthand. (Although I'm delighted to say that when he proposed, I very much wanted to marry him, too.) So to my husband, from the very bottom of my heart: thank you.

And finally, another thank you to you, lovely reader. I wouldn't be here without you. And I hope, in Percy and Cecily, you have found a little more joy in the world.

About the author

Despite the less-than-warm reception of Terri's early stories about cannibal dwarves and talking wolves, she has been writing almost as long as she has been talking. Regency Romance is her passion, fed on a diet of Georgette Heyer and Julia Quinn, and she especially loves an irredeemable rake. By day, she's a ghostwriter, but don't ask her about it because if you did, she'd have to kill you.

She lives in England with her sadly redeemable husband and the love of her life (her dog). When she's not writing, she's probably wishing she was.

Printed in Great Britain
by Amazon

62806475R00092